USA *TODAY* BESTSELLING AUTHOR

Dale Mayer

MAN DOWN

MASON'S MARK

MASON'S MARK: MAN DOWN, BOOK 6
Beverly Dale Mayer
Valley Publishing Ltd.

ISBN-13: 978-1-778866-27-2
Print Edition

Books in This Series:

Jasper, Book 1
Masters, Book 2
Gideon, Book 3
Tristan, Book 4
Guilliam, Book 5
Mason's Mark, Book 6

About This Book

There is no greater motive than bloodlust, DNA, and revenge mixed up in a cocktail of hatred …

Grateful to be alive, Mason knows he owes his friends and family not only for his life but for protecting his wife and unborn child. When he realizes that it might not be completely over, he's on guard, yet not capable enough to defend his family, so he must rely on those around him.

Tesla can't believe it's over. Mason will make it. They have gotten to the bottom of who targeted him and why, … right? It's over surely. Until Janelle calls in a panic, crying out a warning, and Tesla realizes to what extent deep pockets, empty promises, and the vow of revenge can drive one person.

Tesla will do anything to keep her family whole and safe. No one—and she means *no one*—will take that from her now …

Sign up to be notified of all Dale's releases here!
https://geni.us/DaleNews

PROLOGUE

G UILLIAM AND JANELLE headed to his car, walking past the remnants of her mother's house. Janelle stopped and stared, feeling the tears well up in her eyes. Yet resolutely she turned and walked away. She caught sight of the gun-toting arsonist, stooping to get into the back of a cruiser. Something about the angle of his face, the expression on his face, got her attention. She froze, not exactly sure why it seemed familiar.

Beside her, Guilliam nudged her and said, "Come on. It's over. We can buy you a change of clothing, then go home, get a shower, clean up, and maybe grab a few more hours of sleep." As they neared his vehicle, the other team members were gathered there—Masters, Gideon, Evan, and Jasper.

Janelle shook her head. "I won't sleep now."

Evan snorted. "Yeah, neither will I." He faced Guilliam and said, "I think I'll just head out, if you guys are okay with that, unless you think you need me still." He turned to look at each man, then at Guilliam again. All the men shook their heads.

"Wait," she called out, then frowned. "I know this will sound horribly strange, but—"

"But what?" Jasper asked.

"Evan, would you do me a favor?"

"Sure. What is it?"

"Go to the hospital. Something doesn't feel right ..." She stumbled over the words.

All the men stopped to face her. "Why?" asked Jasper.

"I don't know. I'm hoping it'll come to me, but just something is there."

Evan nodded. "I wanted to check in with Tesla anyway. I'll grab a change of clothes and head over to the hospital. Will that work?"

She nodded and smiled. "Thank you."

"That's okay. You just owe me another meal." And, with that, he took off, chortling to himself.

She looked over at Guilliam, as he helped her to his car. "I like your friends," she shared, with a big smile.

He smiled back at her. "Good, but they're also *your* friends. You've known both Evan and Tesla for a long time. You've met some more good people here, and they will love you just as much as I do."

She shook her head. "Even knowing what I did?"

"Of course. Nobody judges you for looking after your mother."

"Just me," she whispered.

"And you shouldn't either," he stated. "Now come on. Let's get you home. We will have a boatload of hassles to deal with, considering we just lost our wallets and anything else you might have had in your purse that just went up in flames. Luckily I do have some cash at home."

She winced at that. "God, my ID, credit cards, every-thing," she muttered, reality dawning.

"Yep, I know, but it's not the end of the world."

"No, it isn't," she agreed, as she got into the vehicle. She reached for his hand and added, "Not exactly the night I thought we were having."

"No," he said, with a big grin. "Still, we survived yet again, and now it's over."

She nodded, took a deep breath, and whispered, "Is it?"

He asked, "Will you be okay with your house—"

As they drove past her house, she sighed and then nodded. "I think so."

"You only think so?"

"It'll probably take a little bit for it to settle in."

They drove to his home first, so each could get changed out of their smelly smoke-infused clothes. He gave her one of his T-shirts and a pair of shorts, plus flip-flops, way too big, but she had nothing on her feet otherwise. This would do until they got to the store.

As she headed back out to the car, so they could do some shopping for necessities for her, she turned and added, "There's still one thing bugging me."

"Okay. What is that?"

"I don't know," she cried out, "and that's why it's just driving me nuts."

He hesitated. "And you're sure it's important?"

"Yeah, it's very important, but I don't know why, and I don't know what."

"Okay, just think about it while we drive."

She sat back, closed her eyes, and tried to relax. Her life had been a shitshow for hours now, and, as they drove, she thought about the ups and downs of her day. And then it hit her. "Oh my God." Her eyes flew wide open. "It's not over. It's not. Turn this car around. We have to get to the hospital right now."

He stared at her in shock but hit the brakes, already navigating a U-turn. "What do you mean?"

"There will be another attack on Mason and Tesla. I'm sure of it. We need to go. Go, go, go."

And, with that, he went silent and focused on speeding toward the hospital. Once they were headed in the right direction, he asked, "Do you want to explain what this is all about?"

She could barely talk. "Call them. Call them now."

He snatched his phone as they drove to the hospital at hell-bent speeds, punched the last number called, and put the phone on Speaker.

When Evan answered, he asked, "What's going on?"

"Are you at the hospital?" Janelle yelled into the phone.

"Not yet. Why?"

Guilliam replied, "Janelle's in a full-on panic, and we're heading there now."

"Okay," Evan said in a slow tone. "I don't have a problem heading up there right now. I told her that I was going to."

"Yeah, apparently she recognized something."

"Yes," she yelled again. "His face, ... her face, ... the nurse who didn't like me making tea. They have similar features ... Get there, Evan, please! Now!"

CHAPTER 1

MASON OPENED HIS eyes, stared around the hospital room until almost his full view was filled with Tesla's face. He smiled up at her. "Hey," he muttered groggily.

"Hey," she murmured, as she stroked a finger down his cheek. "Am I glad to see you."

He smiled. "Feels like I've been in a fog for a long time."

"In many ways you have," she noted. "You've surfaced. You've gone back under. Sometimes you've surfaced and talked, and what you mentioned made absolutely no sense."

He blinked several times. "Ah, not quite there, was I?"

"No, not quite there," she agreed, with a sad smile.

"What happened? Or have you already told me?"

"I've told you," she noted, "but you need to hear it again." Then she went over it, starting with his stepping off the airplane on the tarmac at the base, only to be taken down by a sniper. This time she saw the comprehension in his gaze, as if he fully understood what she shared.

"Right on the base? A sniper? What distance is that?" he murmured, and she watched as the wheels of his brain churned.

"I'm pretty sure that, while you were out lollygagging around, doing nothing," she teased, "everybody else went to bat to solve this."

"Did they find the shooter?" he asked, his eyes opening again to face her.

"They did," she confirmed, with a smile, "and it's a pretty convoluted story."

He closed his eyes and nodded. "How badly hurt am I?"

"The worst of it was the head injury. The bullet burned into your scalp but bounced off a bone and came out the side of your head," she described, trying to keep her tone casual, but her voice faltered a bit. "So we had to shave off all that beautiful hair."

He gently touched his head and winced. "Still feels like I've got a drummer inside there."

"And you probably will for quite a while," she stated, with a nod, "but you're awake. You're on the mend, and, after what we've been through, I'm very happy to hear you talking again."

"I was talking before, wasn't I?" he asked. His voice sounded like it came from afar. "I seem to remember conversations."

"Yeah, you had conversations and forgot them. You heard a few people talking, but then you would disappear again. We never knew how much you were taking back into the dream state with you."

He studied her face, absolutely loving the full range of emotions in her gaze. "I'm so sorry," he began. "I wouldn't have done that to you by choice."

"I know that," she replied, her smile so full of caring and warmth.

It felt like a hug, just this energy that swept over him. "How long have I been out?"

"Weeks," she stated bluntly.

His eyes flew open at that. "Seriously?"

She nodded. "Yes, weeks, but you're back again now," she declared, with a deep sigh. "So I will let all those weeks go by and not begrudge them one bit."

He studied her face, realizing the trauma she had been through. "I'm so sorry," he murmured again.

She shook her head. "It's fine, Mason. After everything we've been through together? … This is nothing. As long as you're here, and you will stay here, I don't care about any of the rest. I just need you here with me."

He placed his hand gently on her rounded belly. "How's the baby?"

"Baby's doing just fine," she said, smiling, holding his hand against her belly.

"How's Sebastian?"

"He misses us, but his grandfather is keeping him busy and entertained. Everybody is waiting for you to wake up and to be back to your old self."

"I guess that's two separate things, isn't it?"

"It has been, but"—she smiled again—"from the looks of you right now, I would say all that appears to be over with."

"I don't want to say it's over with," he clarified, deep in thought, closing his eyes again. "Yet I am feeling a whole lot more like myself. I'm awake, aware, and may be back to the land of whatever this is," he stated.

"Good," she whispered. "I'll take it."

His lips slipped into a smile again. "Will you tell me who shot me?"

Just then the door opened, and Evan walked in. He looked at Mason, and his face cracked into a huge beaming smile. "Now that's what we want to see," he announced, walking closer. He looked over at Tesla. "Did he just wake up again?"

"Not only just woke up again," she explained, with her face lit up like a Christmas tree, "but this time it appears that he's here to stay."

Evan snorted at that. "Man, did you ever put this gal through it," he muttered. "How could you do such a thing?"

Mason gave him half a smile. "You want to fill me in?"

"Not sure I should," he noted, shaking his head. "The last thing I want is for you to have a relapse."

"Why would telling me what happened cause a relapse?" he asked curiously. "Obviously somebody hates me."

"We thought it would be connected to the military. We thought it would all be some nasty-ass mission gone bad."

"So, it wasn't?" Mason asked, surprise rippling through him. "Just from the little bit that she's told me, a sniper took me out. … I've been trying to figure out who the hell, what terrorist would I have missed on any op?"

Evan nodded, knowing and understanding what Mason was going through. "I'm glad you took it that way because the person who shot you was blackmailed into doing so. Then—to try to get out of it—he made sure he didn't get a good shot."

"Ah, and who was that?"

"Drew Honeycutt."

"Drew," he repeated, frowning at Evan. "I'm not even sure I know any Drew."

"You probably did at one point. I'm not sure if you had much of a relationship. All I can tell you is, he was the sniper."

"Was?"

"Yes, *was*." Evan looked over at Tesla. "How are you

doing?"

"I'm perfect now," she stated, beaming a smile at him.

Mason watched the looks they shared, going back and forth between them. The exchange between them had not gone unnoticed at all by Mason.

Tesla added, "Thanks for asking, Evan."

"Obviously I need to hear an awful lot more about this," Mason pointed out, shifting around in his hospital bed.

"Oh, no you don't," she argued, moving closer. "You're not going anywhere. You're not standing up, and you're not getting out of that bed."

He groaned. "Will you be a bully about this?"

"I absolutely will, if that's what it takes," she stated forcefully. "No way I am letting you get out of bed and into trouble."

"Now, what makes you think I will get into trouble?" he asked, a gentle smile on his face, as she rolled her eyes at him.

"It's *you* we're talking about here," she replied. "If anybody on this planet can find trouble, it's you."

"I usually get out of the trouble just fine."

"Yeah, until a sniper takes you out," she said, not holding anything back, "and, in this case, somebody who knew you."

"Somebody who chose to miss," he added.

"Well, he didn't choose to miss well enough," she snapped.

He squeezed her hand and looked over at Evan. "So, they brought you in on it?"

"Oh, you should see how many of us are in on it," he responded, with a booming laugh. "Yet, for now, just know that it's more than me."

He nodded toward Tesla, who hesitated before she

spoke. "I brought Jasper in."

Mason studied her for a long moment. "And he came?"

"Yeah, he was here already, of course. I think he's taken over the investigative department," she shared, with a rueful smile.

"I'm impressed, if you brought him in," Mason noted. "Somehow you convinced him, and … he ended up taking over because that's what he does."

"He does his job very well," she agreed, "and that's what I needed—somebody who could see everyone here with fresh eyes, somebody who could step in and could handle this nightmare."

"Sounds like you got the answers that you needed," Mason said, an odd look on his face. He turned to Evan and smiled. "Thank you for that."

"That's why I'm here," Evan confirmed. "We think … We think we have all the answers, but …" Evan turned to Tesla, and she nodded her approval. "Janelle seems to think we haven't tied up one last connection."

Tesla shook her head. "There can't be," she countered briskly, sounding a bit too harsh. "How can there be so many people out there affected by this?" she muttered, staring at him in shock.

"She wouldn't tell me. Just told me to get my ass over here."

Tesla chuckled. "What the hell? … And you listened?"

"I did. She was screaming into the phone, so she got my attention. They're also on their way here."

"So, she's expecting what? Another attack?" Tesla asked. "Haven't we gotten to the end of this mess yet?"

"I don't know." Evan rolled his eyes. "I wasn't given much of a choice. I think she was channeling you in a way."

Tesla winced at that and then burst out laughing. "The fact that Janelle and Guilliam will be back together again is huge. You didn't know them back then," she added, looking from one man to the other, "but they were perfect together."

Mason, his voice soft, whispered, "Are they back together?"

She looked over at him and nodded. "We have lots to fill you in on, but one thing you need to know is that Janelle's mother passed away yesterday."

Mason closed his eyes as he processed that. "Which is why Guilliam is back in her life."

"Exactly, and what nobody knew is that Janelle's mother has been in contact with him from the very beginning, … asking him to just hold on so that she could have her daughter for a little bit longer, until she got through the worst of her chemo. What nobody realized at the time was that there was no getting over it."

"Right," Mason muttered. "Cancer, wasn't it?"

"Yes, breast cancer that had metastasized to her lungs."

"In that case, how come they are back at it already? Janelle should be home taking care of herself."

"That's one hell of a story too. Within minutes of her mother's passing, Janelle was kidnapped by Greg, cousin to Gabe, the man you killed when he invaded your home and tried to hurt Tesla."

"I remember him," Mason growled.

Evan stepped in and continued. "Janelle was bundled up and smuggled out through the laundry, right here at the hospital, and held in a van outside in the parking lot, where Greg used her to try to coerce Guilliam to come in and finish … killing you, in exchange for Janelle's life."

Mason's gaze widened at that. "Good God, you guys

have been having fun."

"I don't think *fun* is quite the word I would use," Guilliam argued from the door, as he stepped forward with Janelle right beside him, both looking like hell. "Obviously," he added, sauntering in, "I turned down the invitation."

Mason smiled at him. "You have my thanks for that."

"No thanks needed." Guilliam walked over to the hospital bed and closed his hand over Mason's and gave it a gentle squeeze. "How are you doing?"

"I'm awake and apparently more lucid than I've been to date. Yet waking up has caused all kinds of information to float around me, and I'm not sure I'm grasping it all yet."

"I wouldn't be at all surprised. Not only that, some pretty significant events have happened since you were hit," he shared. "I think we've got, what?" He frowned at Tesla, then Evan, and back to Mason. "Four, five, dead, I believe. With four and counting in custody. We're here now … because Janelle doesn't think we're through."

Janelle smiled at Mason, then walked over to Tesla and gave her a gentle hug. "Are you okay?"

"I'm doing fine," she replied. "Now what's this about you thinking it's not over?"

Janelle looked like hell and still smelled like she'd come from a campfire. "I just got this incredible panicked feeling that you were in danger, that Mason was in danger."

Tesla stared at her friend intently, refraining from interrupting her.

"It feels foolish while I'm standing here with you now," she admitted, "but, all I can tell you is that I thought I saw a connection between … What was his name?" She turned to Guilliam.

He relented and replied, "Steve."

Jasper entered the room at that moment and looked at the team already gathered around the bed. He went on to greet Tesla and then came over to Mason. "Welcome to the land of the living. You gave us quite a scare."

"Sorry, but it looks like I'm back … and for real this time."

"It's high time, and I'm pretty damn glad, for many reasons."

"So, I heard the name, … Steve," Mason repeated, rolling the name around. "I'm not sure I have a Steve coming to mind who would make any sense in this sniper scenario."

"He mostly worked in the investigative office."

"Aah, the one that Jasper is now running?" Mason asked.

Guilliam looked at him expectantly. "You heard about that already, *huh?* Yes, so I was tracking the grandson, which led to the kidnapping of Janelle, then the fire."

"Fire? Is that what I smell? What grandson? … I must have missed something." Mason looked perplexed.

Jasper pulled out a chair and sat down beside him. "Greg is the grandson of Richard, two persons of interest," he explained. "An awful lot of information is flying around, and it'll just get more convoluted as the story gets told. So, I don't expect you to get it all at once. I know you will have a million questions, so I'm thinking the best way to go about it is to sit down and go through all of it, at least the highlights, from the beginning."

And, with that, Jasper, slowly and as succinctly as he could, gave Mason a summary of everything that had gone on since he'd been hit.

When Jasper finally got through the bulk of it, Mason stared from one to another. "Damn. All because of Gabe invading my home?" His gaze went quickly to Tesla, sitting there with her hand over her mouth. "That little bastard was planning on raping and torturing her right in front of me," Mason snapped, his voice gaining in volume, "and somebody thinks that we're to blame for that piece of shit dying?" He shook his head. "Christ."

HE SHIFTED UNEASILY in the bed, clearly unsettled. Looking at the machines tracking his vitals, Tesla moved closer to his side. "If you get upset, I'm kicking them all out."

He smiled at her. "Soon enough," he conceded, looking at the others in the room. "I still need more information."

"More information can wait," Jasper stated, studying him. "You need more time to assimilate everything you've just been told."

"Maybe so," Mason admitted. "This is all just ... It sounds so far-fetched."

"Exactly," Tesla agreed, "especially to think it wasn't because of one of your missions. We've been cross-checking information left, right, and center. I've been searching through op files, looking for anything to give us even a hint or some way to find out who was behind this. Then I find out it was a cousin of Gabe's, the asshole who broke into our home," she explained, her bottom lip trembling.

Guilliam nodded slowly, then turned back to Jasper. "Do you think it's over?"

"We would like to say for sure that it's over, but, so far, I am not certain we can say that."

Mason let his eyelids drift slowly closed. "Okay. And do we have any idea who else could possibly be involved?"

"I think we do," Janelle stated, "but ..."

Mason looked over at her and smiled. "Now's not the time to be shy. If you have any suspicions, then you need to bring it up. Nobody here will judge you if you're wrong."

She hesitated, looking over at Guilliam.

He took her hand in his. "You were worried, and we ran over here. You had Evan heading here too. So you had a sense that something was off, that something was still wrong. So never hesitate to speak up to save one of us. Instincts are a huge part of the work we all do, and those instincts frequently make no sense at all, but we've been saved by them too. So we all get it. Therefore, if you feel a piece of this is unresolved, let's hear it."

She nodded, then began, "All I can tell you is that our arsonist, Steve, looked very familiar to me. I think he looks like somebody on the hospital staff."

They all just stared. "You think he's related to a hospital staff member?"

"Yes, that's exactly what I think."

"And you're thinking that, because of that relationship, Mason's still in danger?" Tesla asked, now right at her friend's side.

Janelle turned to her friend and nodded. "Sorry. ... I wish I didn't feel that way, but I do. That's why I made Evan come straight here."

Evan nodded. "If you're right," he replied, deep in thought, "that would make sense." He looked over at Jasper. "We have Steve's last name. Let's run him against the hospital staff list and see if we get any hits. That's an easy-enough check."

Janelle sighed. "I will feel like an absolute idiot if I'm wrong."

"Her last name may not be a match due to marriage or

the paternal line versus the maternal line. All that doesn't matter," Guilliam stated. "Half of our business and our process is sorting through information, deciding what we keep, what we get rid of, what fits, and what doesn't," he shared, calming her down. "You've given us that tidbit. Now just leave it with us. We'll see if we can find anything else."

Tesla looked over at her and smiled. "At least you thought of it." She patted her hand. "You can bet that, from now on, I'll be extremely wary of all the hospital personnel."

"Ha. You've been extremely wary right from the beginning."

"Of course," she admitted, not looking away. "When you have something so precious, you don't let anybody take it away from you, not without a fight." Tesla's gaze went from Janelle to Guilliam and back.

Janelle nodded. "I agree, and I'm not letting him go anytime soon."

"Not ever," Guilliam countered, looking at her. "Please tell me *not ever*."

She laughed. "Not ever," she declared.

Tesla smiled. "You have no idea how happy that makes me." She took another glance at the monitors reading Mason's vitals. "Guys, he is definitely tiring, so it's probably best if you step back out of the room. The nurses will be coming in soon, and, once they see he's awake, the doctors are sure to be ordering all kinds of tests."

Mason groaned. "All kinds of torture, more like it. Nothing quite like being in a hospital."

Evan smiled cheerfully. "Which also means there's nothing quite like getting your ass better, so you can get out of here. And soon too."

Mason smiled up at him. "I'll do my best."

"I know you will," Evan noted. "Now we will go off and check out some things. We have two guards outside your door and another pair nearby. So, Mason, you don't need to worry about that."

"Got it," he replied, as his eyes drifted closed.

Evan added, "Plus, Janelle and Guilliam, you two need to stick close by and watch every hospital employee who enters this room."

Everyone knew what they had to do and shared a nod with each other, then another for Tesla.

She watched everybody leave. Then she got up and closed the door behind them, checking to make sure the guards were there as she did so. She sat down at Mason's side.

"I'm right here."

CHAPTER 2

T HE NEWS WAS both good and terrible. Good in the sense that the team had finally gotten to this point, and terrible in the sense that somebody else within the investigative office had been involved. Yet Tesla could see why, from Janelle's point of view, something was still very off here. And to think that whoever triggered Janelle was someone here on staff at the hospital—including nurses, doctors, or anyone on the premises—made Tesla even more suspicious.

She stepped outside, saw the guards, and quickly phoned Jasper. "Can you send me a photo of this Steve guy?"

"Okay. … What are you thinking?"

"I just want to see what he looks like. At least then, if I see a family resemblance, like Janelle did, I can be a little more discerning, when anybody comes in Mason's room."

"Will do," Jasper noted. "Give me five."

When she finally got the photo, she studied it for the longest time, but it meant nothing to her. The face didn't mean anything—the features, nothing. She sat back and looked over at Mason, but he was sound asleep.

She wrapped her arms around her belly, so damn grateful that Mason was awake and talking, and this time he appeared lucid. To be fair, he had appeared lucid a couple times before, but, when he woke up again later, he seemed to have no memory of the earlier conversations.

The doctors told her that was normal and to just give his brain a chance to recuperate. She was prepared to give his brain all the time it needed. She just wanted to ensure he lived. She didn't want to contemplate life without him. They had built something so special together, and she wanted to hold on with both hands. The thought of losing him was more than she could bear. She sat here, her arms wrapped around her belly, just rocking back and forth. He'd asked about the baby, but she doubted he had any idea of the due date for this one. She was still quite a few weeks away, but these weeks in the hospital had been a pretty stressful time, so no one should be at all surprised if the baby arrived early.

Since her firstborn, Sebastian, was a boy, she was kind of hoping for a little girl this time, but she would be totally happy to just have a healthy child. It didn't matter, since healthy was what was important. As she stared at her husband, she relaxed a bit, seeing his slow and steady breathing. She smiled, tears in her eyes again, as she thought of how close she'd come to losing him.

Knowing that she had to keep her own stress level under control, she rose and went to the door and asked the guards if it was possible to get a cup of tea.

One of the men smiled at her. "I can go down to the cafeteria and get you something."

She smiled and thanked him, and, as soon as he was gone, she looked over at the other guard. "Is everything okay?"

He nodded. "Everything is fine, but it's best if you stay inside with Mason."

She headed back inside and waited for the tea to arrive.

It shouldn't take very long, but, if the cafeteria was busy, it could easily be half an hour. Since she'd spent all this time waiting, what was a little bit more?

She curled up on her little cot, shifting to get more comfortable. When the door opened, and the guard appeared, she realized it was her tea. She sat up and thanked him profusely.

He smiled. "Don't worry about it." He looked over at the sleeping Mason and muttered, "Damn, it's good to know he's improving."

"Isn't it?" she agreed, with a smile. "He sounded pretty normal and lucid this time."

"Good, though we had never thought anything else," he said, chuckling. "He's always been that way, hasn't he?"

She nodded. "He has. He's one of those guys who you just can't keep down."

"And that's good because we need guys like Mason," the guard noted. "We all need to know that guys like Mason are out there behind us, guys who can take the knocks and who keep coming back."

"That's him. Stubborn and so much more," Tesla agreed.

"I know, for you, it's got to be the hardest thing to deal with," the guard shared, "but, considering how well he's doing, you've got to be feeling better about things."

She nodded. "Yes, it's all pretty amazing." He disappeared back outside the door, and she relaxed. Even though she knew all these men, knowing that some bad guy was still out there, after her and after Mason, well, that was just hard and would keep her on edge.

She trusted these men guarding her and Mason, but the knowledge that somebody still wanted to hurt them was too much to bear. She hoped that the team would quickly get to the bottom of whatever was going on.

It should be over by now. That was the thing that got her. It should be done. They finally got to what they thought was the bottom of it and ended up with so many assholes involved that it was mind-boggling. Yet they were dead or in custody. If Janelle hadn't spoken up about a hospital staff member, Tesla would feel a lot better about things right now. Then again, … what if Janelle didn't mention anything? They would have no idea they were still vulnerable, even in a hospital.

Yet hunches or feelings could be wrong. What if Tesla was upset all over again with no real need to?

Yet what if Janelle was right? That thought popped up in Tesla's head, and she shuddered at the possibility. She sat here, sipping her tea. Then her fatigue washed over her. She sighed, put down her cup, curled up, pulled the blanket over her shoulders, and fell asleep.

MASON WOKE SLOWLY and looked over to see his wife curled up on the small cot beside him. Just thinking of how hard and uncomfortable that cot must be in the very pregnant state she was in, he felt so bad, imagining what she'd been through and how exhausted she must be to even get any sleep on such a contraption. He shifted several more times, getting comfortable himself.

Up until now, every time he woke up, the pain had been located in his head. However, now he recognized the reality that all this time spent unconscious in a hospital bed was harming his body as well. He needed to get moving to the extent that he could. Still, he wouldn't be at all unhappy to get out of here as soon as possible. Yet he also knew that nobody would let him do too much, too quickly. He had no doubts about that.

Everybody had their hospital rules, and understanding them was one thing, but agreeing to comply? … That was entirely different. He smiled as he heard Tesla's gentle breathing beside him. She always had the cutest way of sleeping, curled up in a ball.

He used to spoon right around her and the two of them could sleep like that for hours. Based on what he had learned earlier, he'd slept for hours and hours these last few weeks, and even now the news they had shared with him was mind-boggling.

He couldn't imagine how this had all come about or how anybody was left to come after him. It's not that he would ever disregard Janelle's thoughts—or anyone else's for that matter. Yet he sure didn't want to deal with any more people or their betrayals. That always seemed to be the worst thing in his world.

He heard voices out in the hallway, most likely his guards, the nurses, whoever. Hospitals seemed like a never-ending stream of people, poking and prodding, checking on this and that. He had memories, bits and pieces, of talking to various people over the last few days or maybe a week. Yet all those conversations were gone, and only pieces remained. He guessed that was why Tesla seemed to be so happy when he was talking.

He couldn't imagine just how traumatic it had all been for her. When she had been hurt, he'd been out of his mind with worry, and he knew it wouldn't be any less for her. He was so sorry she had to go through this. Yet he hadn't had anything to do with it, but still, it pissed him off that somebody would do this to them, to her.

She was the sweetest, nicest woman he'd ever met in his life. The fact that he loved her to distraction just meant he wanted to protect her, but, while unconscious in this bed, that was the last thing he could do.

He opened his eyes again, staring around the room. He still couldn't stay awake very long, and that was guaranteed to drive him nuts as he recuperated. The slowness of his body pulling back into alignment with what he wanted it to do might prove to be his greatest challenge going forward. What he wanted to do was get up and dance with his beautiful wife, but his mind and body weren't yet working together. He smiled at that thought.

"I recognize that smile," she shared. "What are you arguing about now?"

He chuckled. "Not arguing at all," he claimed. "I was just telling my body that we won't handle being in this position for very long, and it needed to heal a whole lot faster than it had so far."

She smiled from her cot, as she looked over at him. "Now *that* sounds very much like my husband." She beamed at him.

He nodded. "Yes, it is very much me," he agreed. "I think the worst thing about being injured is the snail's pace of healing. Just how long is something like this going to keep me in bed?"

"Not just in bed," she clarified, "but you will be off work for a very long time."

He studied her face for a moment and sighed. "Maybe that's okay too."

She gave him the gentlest of smiles. "It is okay. I would

be totally happy to have you spend some time at home with me, Sebastian, and this little one," she shared, her hand resting on her stomach.

Mason's smile widened. "We were planning a long paternity leave anyway," he pointed out.

"We were," she stated, "and who knows? Maybe it will be even longer because of what happened to you."

"It won't be permanent," he declared, staring at her in horror. "No way I could do that."

"I didn't say that. I'm not expecting you to quit your job or anything."

"Good." He closed his eyes, knowing that even the topic would be enough to send him off into a frenzy. "Did everything get shut down up north okay?"

"If you're asking about Mountain, he contacted me just after you were shot to see if he could do anything. I think Jasper even called him in to help with the brass at some point in the midst of this mess."

"Is Mountain doing okay?"

"Yes, he's settling in with his new situation and his new partner, while still dealing with the fallout from that whole op up there."

"Another nightmare," Mason grumbled, with a deep breath, "a nightmare that should never have happened."

"I know," she whispered. "Of course Mountain's brother, Teegan, has quite a bit of recovering to do too. It's been a tough one for everybody."

"Especially Teegan. Then I no sooner get home and *boom*. I'm down." He shook his head. "Seems like we've had some pretty shitty months."

"We have," she agreed, "so we're due for some good ones, and the fact that you are back here with me now? …

I'll take them."

He chuckled. "I am a bit hungry," he said, giving her a fading smile.

"Are you sure about that?" she asked intently. "Or is it just you telling your body to wake up and to get with the program because you have plans?"

He glared at her in mock anger. "Now would I do that?"

"Absolutely," she declared in a dry tone. "No doubt about it. I believe you would do nearly anything you could think of to push yourself back into shape." She spoke with a broad smile on her face.

He sagged back on the pillows. "It almost sounds like me."

"Right? It's almost as if I know you," she teased, with a smile. "And it's all good because you won't be doing anything crazy right now because you can't."

"And you're enjoying that just a little too much," he quipped in a mocking tone.

"No, no," she countered, "but what I am enjoying … is the fact that you're awake, that you can talk, and that you have your brain cells truly functioning. For a while there, I wasn't so sure."

He sighed. "That is probably the scariest part of all this," he noted. "When I think of what a brain injury can do to somebody, it freaks me out just a little."

"Exactly, but, just because you're doing better, we won't get carried away," she stated, "which is also why I want to ensure that you don't try going anywhere, not even to the en-suite bathroom, not until they say you can." He winced at that, but she shook her head. "No, sir, you're not taking one step out of that bed until the doctor gives you the go-ahead."

He glared at her. "I don't do sickness well."

"I do know that," she replied, "and the doctors did say that it was a good sign that your body was healing as fast as it was, but they still want to see your brain healing as well."

"Hey, I was just taking a time out," he explained. "While I was doing that, my body and brain were healing. So, once I get back on my feet again," he added coyly, "you can expect me to be completely back."

She just stared at him, then slowly shook her head. "Nice try."

He groaned but added, "You'll see."

"Yeah, I sure will," she muttered under her breath, "but, for now, you can just stay put and take some time to adjust to being awake."

He smiled at her. "I love you too." Tears came to her eyes, and he whispered, "Damn, I'm so sorry about all this, honey."

"I know," she muttered, wiping back the tears. "It's just not fair that this happened at all, but especially not when I'm pregnant. I've been an emotional wreck."

"Emotional maybe, but still the most beautiful woman I know," he replied.

She burst out laughing at that. "You've always been able to charm the socks off anyone," she stated, with a smile. "I love you for saying that. However, the truth of the matter is, I'm very round and huge. I'm super stressed out and most definitely not at my best."

"Are you kidding? You're carrying my child, and you look absolutely beautiful to me."

She got up, walked over, sat down on the bed beside him, and whispered, "Thank you." Then she leaned over and kissed him.

He shifted to the side, moving carefully, so his head didn't move too harshly, then tucked her up beside him on the bed.

She curled up with her arms across his chest, her head resting against his heart, and she whispered, "Seems like forever since I could do this."

"I know," he muttered, tugging her close, carefully trying not to move too quickly. "Feels like a long time since we were in a position to do this, but honestly my head is feeling pretty good. So I vote we do it some more."

"I'm glad to hear that," she said, with a smile, "but I'm still not letting you get up."

He groaned. "You will keep me in bed the whole time, won't you?"

"If we were at home, and I wasn't eight months' pregnant, I might agree to that"—she rolled her eyes—"but right about now, I just want to see you healthy."

He cuddled her close and whispered, "Let's go back to sleep, and that's what I will do."

"I would love to," she shared, "but not like this. You won't get any sleep this way." She shifted upward slowly. "Now get some rest."

"Will you tell me when they check in?"

"I will," she agreed.

"It won't take them very long to read through the employee roster, right?"

"It won't take them long for that, but it will take a little bit of time for anything else," she pointed out. "So don't expect answers. I've been waiting for weeks to get this far, remember?" He winced at that. "Sometimes it just doesn't happen that easily."

"No, it's not easy or fast, but still, we do the best we can."

"Now you get some sleep." Then she kissed him again and moved over to her cot.

CHAPTER 3

TESLA WOKE WITH a start and then moaned, as the baby kicked the crap out of her lower back. Tesla shifted in her cot, twisting to confirm everything in the room was okay. She was so damn grateful that Mason had recovered enough to be conscious for longer periods of time, yet she would love to get both of them home and in their own bed. Yesterday she had taken a couple moments and gone home, showered, and changed, only to come back to her husband's side.

Even for that brief amount of time, she was loathe to leave him. Yet, with him on the mend, it should be okay. However, everything inside her screamed at her to not leave him again.

She hated that because, in the face of everything else going on, it just meant that she didn't feel that it was over. Despite having security in place, it wasn't safe to leave Mason just yet. He was better, no doubt about it, much better, but he was not capable of fending off an attack, and that meant he should not be left alone. She had contemplated the thought of bringing the guards into the hospital room and going home for a few hours of sleep, which wouldn't be a bad idea, unless of course Mason was attacked in the meantime.

As far as the rest of the team was concerned, if Tesla and Mason were attacked in this hospital room, it's not as if she could do a whole lot about it, and she hated that premise. Because of her pregnant state, she would be even more vulnerable and potentially not as good of a protector of her husband as she would want to be. It was the sad compromise when you had a baby to protect and the unwieldy pregnant body that went with it.

She shifted in her cot once again, then realized her bladder wouldn't let her go back to sleep. She slowly made her way out of bed and crept toward the bathroom. When she was done, she turned off the light and opened the door to hear Mason, his tone quiet, as he whispered, "Couldn't you sleep?"

"Your child decided to kick my bladder one too many times," she shared, with a note of humor.

He whispered right back, "Come cuddle with me, and maybe you'll go back to sleep again."

"Maybe, but you wouldn't get any rest at all," she noted, with a groan. "As much as I absolutely would love to spoon with you, it's just not good for you."

He groaned softly. "It would be nice if you weren't quite so protective."

She chuckled as she walked closer and stared down at him, the moonlight gleaming through his window. "I just want to get you well enough to go home," she stated, "and honestly, I would love to go home myself."

He hesitated and then nodded. "That's the thing, isn't it? It's not just me. We need to get you and baby home, where you're more comfortable."

"And that's true, but don't even start thinking that will

be the excuse to get you out of here too early."

"It is an excuse," he admitted, with a smile, "and I will try it with the medical personnel. Besides, we can get medical assistance at home, so it's not a risk."

"You're not going anywhere for at least a few more days," she pointed out. "If we can make it happen after that, then fine, but only if the doctor says so."

"*Hmm,*" he muttered. "even having security guards here has got to be disruptive for them."

"I don't care if it's disruptive or not," she stated firmly. "First things first, and that is getting you back on your feet. In the meantime, we've got to keep you safe, hence the guards. So they're not going anywhere."

He chuckled softly. "Who knew you were such a tigress?"

"You knew," she declared, with a sigh of her own. "Honestly, I think it's one of the reasons you married me."

"No. I married you because I couldn't stand the thought of life without you."

Tears caught in the back of her throat at his words. She reached for him, her belly bump getting in the way. He chuckled as she shifted, so he slowly sat up and reached his arms around her. "You need to go back to sleep," she murmured.

"I'm fine," he said. "I know you'll protect me."

"Yes," she interrupted. "And now that you're awake, you'll take over that role," she conceded, "but you aren't healthy enough to do it yet." He was silent for a moment, but she could almost sense Mason's frown in the darkness, and she chuckled. "I know. You don't want to be talked to like that."

"It's not so much that I don't want to hear that," he clarified, followed by his own laugh, "but it's hard to think that you're suffering, while I've got the only bed."

"I have a bed," she said, with a wave of her hand, "and I added some soft foam on top to help protect my back."

"It's not the same."

"No, it sure isn't," she agreed cheerfully. "It's not the same thing, but it's also not an issue. Remember, depending on how it goes, it may be just a few more days until you can go home to recover. Then we can both go home. Maybe we can get a nurse in or something at home."

"A nurse?" he repeated in horror.

She wanted to laugh at the tone in his voice. If ever a horror was to be had, to Mason it was apparently the prospect of having a nurse at home, and she knew no way in hell would that work well. Mason would make the nurse and everybody else nearby miserable. "At some point you just have to accept that your body needs some healing."

"Sure," he replied, with a sigh, "and it's getting healing right now, but the sooner I can get my ass home again—"

"Which I'll say again is not happening soon," she interrupted.

"Oh, I get it. Even if it's another six weeks of bed rest at home," he shared in that persuasive tone of his, "it's still better than being here."

"I fully agree, but you need a nurse—"

"What for?" he asked, his voice getting loud. They both knew very well what for, but he was frustrated and being difficult.

"Maybe to keep you in line," she snapped.

He went silent again and then chuckled. "I'm fine," he said, with a snort. "I know you're worried, and you don't want me to go too far, too fast, but honestly, Tess, ... being here makes me look weak."

"You've only been truly awake one day, part of one day," she protested. "Give yourself a chance to recover for a moment before you dish out this crap."

"I'll give it one more day," he stated, "but then I want to go home."

"That's nice," she quipped, adding an eye roll, as she stepped farther away to sit on her cot.

"Are you sure you're feeling okay?" he asked.

"I'm feeling fine," she murmured, "absolutely fine."

"Good enough. I guess I have to trust you on that."

"You absolutely do," she snapped at him again. "Just like I've been looking after you for these last weeks"—she sighed deeply—"I am looking after our unborn baby."

"I would expect nothing less," he whispered. "Now I'm thinking we could both use a little more sleep."

"Sounds good to me," she agreed, as she yawned. "I swear that's the one thing that's hard about being pregnant. You never can get enough sleep. And don't even bother to say it because I'm not going home where I might get a bit more."

"Another reason why I need to get better faster," he pointed out. "At least then we can get you home, where you can get some quality rest and where I can stand watch over you instead."

"Yeah, that's not happening for a while yet," she muttered, with a note of humor.

"What if I want to talk to one of the guards outside?" he asked curiously.

She opened her eyes, raised herself up on one elbow, and stared at him. "I suppose you could, ... as long as you don't expect to con them into breaking you out of here."

He burst out laughing. "Now that sounds like a great idea, but it's okay. I promise I'll take you with me."

She rolled her eyes and collapsed back down again. "Just don't wake me up while you're getting in trouble." Then she rolled over, pulled the blanket up over her shoulders, and crashed.

MASON WOKE UP as if coming out of layers of clouds. He was sure a lot of the problems he was still dealing with were a result of the medications he was on. Still, the medications helped to reduce the brain swelling and helped to heal the damage to the cranial bone. He knew he needed time, recuperation time, but it was also hard when he saw his beloved wife suffering as much as she was, though she wouldn't be happy with him for putting her comfort ahead of his recovery.

It almost felt as if he'd taken way too long to get to this point, and now he needed to blast through the rest of this healing so he could get back to a normal life. Even if it wasn't quite back to his former normal life, he needed to get back to something much closer than this.

A few minutes later the door opened, and a doctor walked in. Mason looked up and smiled. "Just the man I wanted to see," he said cordially.

The doctor raised his eyebrows and shook his head. "Don't even bother asking to go home." When Mason narrowed his gaze, the doctor just laughed. "You think I haven't seen guys like you before?"

"Ah, you are one of those …"

"Yep. I'm Dr. Casper, and I know what you think. You

think you're made of titanium, and then somebody comes along and pops a hole in that steel. You guys are perfect model patients, as long as you're unconscious," he noted in a dry tone. "Yet the minute you're awake, that's it. All hell breaks loose, and, as far as you're concerned, you should be entitled to leave as soon as possible."

"Absolutely I should be," Mason confirmed. "You do see the condition my wife is in, right?"

"I do," the doc said, with a smile. "I also know that she's been a model patient herself. So, as long as we feel you need to be here, she'll be all for it."

"Sure, but I also need to get home," he pointed out.

"As soon as I get some more tests run, now that you're awake, we'll discuss a realistic time frame for release and what that might look like. In the meantime, nope, nada, no way. You're not going anywhere." He quickly ran through some questions, got to the reality of how Mason felt, then he ran through a few other checks. Finishing up, he added, "Even though I said that you couldn't go home, and I haven't changed my mind on that"—he raised his hands to stop Mason—"considering the severity of your condition, you are doing surprisingly well."

"No surprise about it," Mason declared. "I'm doing very well and want to go home."

"We'll still run you through some tests. I'll order those now, and we'll see how you're doing afterward. Meanwhile you require bed rest before going home."

"And that's fine," Mason conceded. Now that he'd gotten his point through to the doctor, plus heard a note of positivity, he wouldn't push it. He looked back over to see Tesla had her eyes open and wore an expression of surprise.

She asked the doctor, "Did you just say he could go

home?"

"No, I most certainly did not," the doctor clarified, turning to give her a smile. "I just mentioned that he is healing quite well. We will run him through another battery of tests to see how the brain is healing. Even when he does go home, he will be ordered to continue bed rest to heal at home," he stated, looking from one to the other.

Tesla nodded. "Got it."

"Even if he is discharged, … we are looking at regular checkups, mandatory bed rest, and he must be off work until further notice, no physical activity, the whole nine yards. Do you hear me?" he asked, turning to look at Mason.

"I hear you," Mason replied.

Dr. Casper just rolled his eyes. "You would claim to hear anything, as long as you thought it would get you home."

"You could be right," Mason admitted, with a smile. "Besides, it's not as if you guys don't have plenty of other uses for the beds here."

"Unfortunately, that's the truth," he muttered, with a sigh. "As soon as we get ourselves caught back up and get some of the bed numbers down, they just fill right back up again. Anyway, we'll talk tomorrow, and hopefully we will have some test results back." And he turned and headed out.

Feeling immensely better, Mason looked over at Tesla and grinned.

She shook her head. "I don't have a clue how you managed to do that."

"Hey, he could see the sense of it. Besides, once I'm at home, I'll rest better."

"Maybe," she conceded, "but that doesn't mean I will though. I will be constantly waking up to confirm you are still in bed." When he frowned, she shrugged. "Plus, I don't know that this mess is over with."

"The men have another twenty-four hours to get it together," he noted cheerfully, "and, if we need security at the house, then we'll have security at the house." She frowned. "It's not as if they aren't our friends anyway," he pointed out.

"Very true," she replied cautiously. "I'm just surprised that you're willing to give in that much."

"I'm not giving in to anything," he declared, looking at her. "I'm just making things work."

She rolled her eyes at that. "Your idea of making things work generally means you're in control."

He chuckled. "You could be right."

She smiled. "I am right about it, and you won't change. Still, if truth be known, I don't want you to."

"Good enough," he agreed. "So, as long as we understand each other, there's no problem."

"Only if the doctor clears you."

He nodded. "Honestly, I won't take much of a chance anyway," he said, smiling at her. "My brain is a little too important."

"Yeah, and somebody gave it a good poke," she muttered.

"I still find that quite surprising, that and everything else they've sorted out since the sniper shooting."

"Too bad they didn't quite get it finished."

"I'm not sure they didn't," he shared. "They've come a long way, and it was a very convoluted path."

"Very, but that doesn't mean it's over yet."

"You keep saying that."

She nodded. "I guess I've just been worried for so long that I don't know how to let it go."

"That makes sense." Shuffling back in the bed, Mason added, "Sounds like I will be gone for a few hours for these tests."

"In that case, I might go home and take a shower, get changed, pull out a change of clothes for you too, and come back again."

Mason suggested, "You could stay there all day, you know?"

She smiled. "I'll see, but I'll be back later this afternoon because I want to hear the test results."

"Oh, come on." Maon groaned. "Are you suggesting I can't be trusted to give you a complete and honest report?"

She rolled her eyes at that. "If you thought it would get you out of this place, there is no telling what you might do."

He burst out laughing. "Maybe so, but I would never lie to you."

"Good enough," she said, as a nurse came along soon afterward with an orderly, and Mason was wheeled away, his guards going with him.

She would have preferred he was in a wheelchair. Still, it was wonderful to see him sitting up like that. Something about being bedridden made such a difference. Seeing someone standing or even sitting up made them look so much more alive. Not a great thing to say, but it was true.

She packed up her things and stepped outside the room. "Hey, Evan. You're still here?" she asked.

"I am at the moment," he said, with a nod. "What are you up to?"

"Mason's gone for some tests, and the doctor told me that it will be a couple hours." She shrugged. "So I thought I would go home and have a shower and get a change of clothes for me and Mason. And, who knows, maybe even close my eyes and get a cat nap in my own bed," she added, with half a smile.

"I'm coming with you," he said, as he pulled out his phone.

She asked, "Why?"

"No whys allowed," he replied. "I'm coming, and that's all there is to it. If you want to go home, you go home with me in tow."

She closed her mouth, thought about it, then shrugged. "I guess after all this, it makes no sense to fight it."

"Exactly," he stated, with a nod. "I'm also making sure we have somebody here for when Mason gets back." She waited while he made the arrangements, and then he asked, "You want to leave right now?"

She sighed. "I could wait if I need to, but I was hoping to go now," she shared, as she reached around to massage her lower back.

"That's fine," Evan noted. "Just give me five."

She nodded. "It'll take me that long to get to the bathroom and back."

He burst out laughing as she headed back inside to the bathroom. When she came back out, he was talking with Markus. She gasped in delight as he opened his arms, and she waddled over and gave him a hug. "Have you been out here all the time too?"

"Just like everybody else," Markus stated casually, "we've been taking turns. It's wonderful to hear he's going for tests and potentially will get out of here."

"He'll still need help for quite a while," she said.

"That's fine, as long as he's doing well. By the looks if it, he's improving in leaps and bounds. He's back on track, so don't get despondent over that."

"I'm not, but you should hear him griping though." Both men grinned. "See? That's the thing. You guys are all the same. The minute somebody says you can't go anywhere, do something, plus you have to follow rules, you get your backs up."

Markus and Evan both nodded and grinned like fools. "But not out of stubbornness," Evan pointed out. "It's more because it's not what we're used to."

"Sure, but sometimes it doesn't matter what you're used to. You just have to shut up and get with the program, regardless."

Markus smiled, looking from Evan back to her. "I hear you're going home for a bit?"

"Yes, I was hoping to for a few hours to shower and whatnot. I'll also get some clothes for Mason. He may not need them, but you know how it is."

"Oh, nice. I'm sure he'll appreciate that."

"You both know all too well about hospital gowns and being bedridden. They don't do a whole lot for our psyche, and Mason is, ... well, just Mason."

"Yeah, the hospital gown is not good for anyone," Markus agreed, with a smile. "So, Evan will look after you."

She smiled her thanks and added, "I don't know how we'll ever pay back you guys for doing all this." She was getting emotional at the thought of how many of them had stepped up to look after them.

Markus shook his head. "There's no paying back for something like this. We're family, remember?"

Still choking back the tears, she nodded. "We are."

Markus added, "And I'll be here, waiting for Mason to return."

Tesla nodded and waved, as she quickly made her way

over to Evan, and they headed down to the parking lot.

Evan asked her, "Do you want to take your car?"

"Are you bringing me back to the hospital?"

"Definitely," he said, with a nod.

"In that case, then you can drive," she muttered, even as she wiped away the tears. "Nothing like being pregnant to get emotional all the time."

"And nothing like having your family tossed into the soup like this to get emotional too," he added. "Yet what Markus said was right. He meant it, and so do I."

"Thank you," she whispered.

He laughed. "It's all good, and the fact that Mason will not only make it but end up okay, that is huge."

"I know," she whispered, "and, after everything, it's all been so traumatic."

"Which is also why we're keeping the guards up until we know for sure that we've gotten to the bottom of this."

"How do we know that?" she asked, turning to look at him. "I hear what you guys are saying, and in theory it sounds wonderful, but how do we really know if that will be the end of it?"

"Meaning, how will we know for sure?"

"Yeah," she said. "How will we know for sure?"

He pondered that before speaking. "I guess when we've filled in all the cracks and when we know that any other crime is accounted for, especially with a suspect who fits the bill."

"But how do we know there isn't still one more person out there, dying to do this old man's bidding?"

"Why would they?" he asked, looking at her.

She thought about it and said, "How about money, love, and power? How about sheer retribution?"

"Oh, we've got the grandfather's bullying and blackmailing and retribution, which is all about power. We've got money, which is why the grandson Greg was doing Richard's bidding. So what's missing?" he asked, looking at her curiously.

"Love," she whispered. "There is love, but who would love such a cruel and bitter old man like Richard?"

"His wife is long gone."

"I know," she said, "and maybe nobody loved him. Maybe that's part of the problem. Maybe it's more about hate, revenge."

"We're still on alert, and I'm not so much worried about missing some person," Evan shared, "not until a few more days go by. Then we can better know if somebody else is involved."

Tesla shuddered at some related thought. "Even at that, I don't know that we can ever be sure."

It wasn't long before she was inside her house and felt a huge sense of homecoming. Her shoulders sagged in instant relief.

Evan smiled at her. "Nothing quite like it, is there?"

"No." She looked around her home. "There isn't." She quickly dropped her bags and tried to stretch unsuccessfully, then just gave up. "I'm heading for a shower."

He nodded. "Do you mind if I put on some coffee?"

"Go for it," she said. "None for me though. I've already had my allotted coffee for the day."

"I could put on the kettle for you."

"I'll do it when I get out of the shower," she murmured.

She headed up and had a quick shower. When she came back downstairs, fully dressed again, she had several changes of clothing in her bag and a new bag as well.

"How many bags do you have now? You didn't even take the old one up with you."

"I know," she agreed, with a wave of her hand. "You may think that you're prepared for something like this, but you're not. I picked up several bags this time, as I packed a couple changes of clothing for me and now for Mason. I put the laundry on hold and just take care of things as I go along." She frowned at him and added, "There's something very different this time though."

"I suppose it's a whole different deal with Mason doing so much better. It's enough that he's awake and talking, but the idea that he could be out of there in a matter of days is amazing."

"It's unbelievable, I know," she said, with a bright smile. She busied herself, putting on laundry and getting everything ready to leave again. "I wouldn't mind a bite to eat. What about you?" she asked, as she walked over to the kitchen and realized not a whole lot was here.

"Yeah, food would be good," Evan replied, with a smile. "I can always eat, but I didn't see much. Sorry, I took the liberty of checking."

"I figured you would, but the cupboards are pretty bare."

"It's not as if you've been here," he noted, looking around the place, "but I found eggs. So we can certainly do omelets. Plus, there's enough for some sandwiches." He rubbed his hands in excitement, already formulating a plan. She knew how much he loved to eat.

He walked over to the pantry and pulled out cans of salmon and tuna, then shrugged back at her.

"Either of those would be good," she said, surprised at the disappointed expression on his face. "Or both," she added, only to be rewarded with his big smile. So that's what they did. By the time they'd been there for a couple hours, she sighed. "As lovely as it's been …"

"I know. You're anxious to get back."

"I am," she murmured, "if you don't mind."

"Of course not, so long as you've got everything you need," he said.

She nodded. "I do, so let's head back to the hospital."

MASON SHIFTED IN his hospital bed with a groan. Nobody was here to hear him, so it was something he could just let out for the first time in a very long time. It was freeing in a way. When a knock came on his hospital room door, he called out, "Come in." Markus walked in, a big smile on his face. "Hey, Markus," Mason greeted him, with a laugh at seeing his old friend. "I've got to tell you, being a patient sucks."

"It does," Markus agreed, "but do you know what sucks worse?"

"I guess you're about to tell me," Mason replied.

"Knowing you might never wake up."

"Ah, crap. Trust you to put it in perspective."

"Yeah, trust me is right," Markus said, with a smile. "Tesla's been through the wringer and back. Things were ugly for quite a while, and just getting you back alive was the dream. Getting you back whole seemed like too much to even hope for."

"I know. I was hoping she would go home and have a real nap in a real bed, but chances are she's probably doing laundry and things like that."

"I think they're already on their way back," Markus noted. "I also heard from Jasper."

Mason narrowed his gaze at him. "And?"

"So far, the grandson Greg is spilling the beans on all this granddad's misdeeds for several decades. The old man acted like some mafia boss, killing people or having them killed just because he wanted to. Greg seems to think that's a fair exchange, now that his grandfather's in jail and not going anywhere and now that Greg's not getting the money his grandfather promised him. It will take a fair bit to confirm that Richard, the grandfather, is behind all these shitty murders because he didn't always pull the trigger himself. Even if so, he'll get a couple dozen murder charges added on his record. Plus, Greg committed some murders himself."

Mason stared at him in shock. "Seriously?"

Markus nodded. "Richard and Greg would both say that their victims weren't even people. Greg tells the story about how his grandfather had an argument with an illegal immigrant who was working for him, and, when the guy wanted to collect his payment for work done, Richard just killed him rather than paying him."

"Crap," Mason muttered. "How the hell has Richard gotten away with it?"

"Early on they lived a long way out, while he built up cattle ranches. Then, as he became more interested in politics and running the town, Richard cleaned up his act somewhat and started hiring thugs to pressure everybody to vote for him. If they didn't, … well, the consequences were severe."

"Damn," Mason muttered in a hard tone. "He's been running amok for a long time."

"And the funny thing is, he stopped when he got too old. He basically just couldn't do anything himself anymore, so he wasn't doing anything that made people afraid of him. The years just went by, and nobody remembered what Richard used to be like. He settled into an anonymity of sorts, where he could do whatever he needed to do on the side. That gave him cover, and, if he was good about it, he got away with it—nothing like he used to when people were around to ask questions. However, when nobody was asking questions, he ran things the way he wanted them."

"Now, he'd been in that old folks' home for what? A good six, seven years?"

"No, it was closer to fifteen, I think. He may have ended up there because he acted up where he was living before—something about trouble with the ladies. He was in that home for decades."

"Of course he would have been difficult with the ladies. That's how we ended up in this mess, isn't it?"

"Yeah, it would seem so."

"Have we tracked down any of those ladies?"

"No, not yet," Markus shared. "We're working on that right now."

"I would be interested in that list," Mason said.

"You think it's important?"

"All the angles are important, but that one would give us some answers. We need to get to the old-timers, as nobody else even knows or understands what he's done. So nobody else has any solid clues or anything to offer."

"Right." Markus frowned.

"If you go the hassled women route, we should track them down to confirm Richard didn't have more kids. Plus, we need to gather a list of any missing persons in Richard's sphere too."

"I think Jasper has the team on it."

"Good enough," Mason said. "Next I need to wrap my head around the idea that somebody in the military may have been behind a sniper shooting me, involving two naval investigators no less—or at least protecting the guy behind it all."

"Yeah, remember how Granddad Richard was former military, so he had his hooks in here too. Oh, yeah, and the brass is having a heyday with that right now too," he shared, with a big grin. "Of course it's also cemented the job Jasper holds now."

"I wonder if he even wants it though," Mason muttered, shaking his head, "I tried to convince him to come out west before, and he wouldn't even consider it."

"Your accident apparently was enough to convince him now." Markus gave Mason a big grin.

"I'm not at all sure that is the case. That would probably have been all about Tesla. She's pretty hard to say no to."

"That woman does know what she wants and how to get it."

"She does, indeed," Mason confirmed, with a gentle smile. "Now the question is, how do we stop whatever the hell is going on right now, so we can all move on with our lives?"

"According to the grandson Greg, he doesn't know anybody else who could be actively involved in his grandfather's revenge tour. Greg thought he was the only one left, and he seemed quite miffed at finding out about Steve possibly being a legitimate son of Richard."

"Of course. How old is this Steve guy?"

"He's right in-between the two grandsons."

"Right, and Richard is no saint, and someone told me that his wife died, leaving him two daughters, when Richard wanted sons."

"Steve confessed—to help reduce the arson and attempted murder charges against him—how he was also promised a fair chunk of change by Richard. Steve's received some money from Richard over the years, unlike the grandson Greg."

"So, what did Greg get?"

"Not much. Greg got his expenses covered but nothing more."

"Granddad was playing the two of them back and forth, *huh*?"

"He was. Whether you like it or not, Steve had spunk, and he got away with shit."

"He got away with too much shit," Mason declared. "Any chance of his being Richard's secret son? One that wouldn't be above squeezing good ole dad for cash in exchange for silence?"

"Considering that Steve's fortysomething today, then Richard was old even back then to father Steve. Still, forty years ago people could get away with all kinds of stuff that you would like to think they couldn't get by with now."

"Maybe they can't, or maybe they still can, and we just haven't caught them."

"I would like to think not," Markus stated, with a snort. "An awful lot of us are on this right now, making sure we get the last of it wrapped up."

Mason nodded.

Markus added, "I can get the list of potential women together who could be Steve's mom, but it'll only be conjecture for the most part. So far nothing points to anyone working at the hospital—at least not someone with Steve's last name." He frowned at that.

"Richard was forced to change nursing homes about fifteen years ago, right?" Mason asked. "That randy old geezer could have plenty of offspring, some which he may not even be aware of. Plus, at this point, we're working on people's fading memories and even the gossip from back in the day, whether fifteen years ago or forty. That will make getting any viable information that much harder to confirm with a second source."

Markus suggested, "If the naval database is up to date, we might find Richard's DNA. If so, we could compare it to Steve's. Jasper has got the team checking on that as well."

Mason shook his head. "But we already have an inkling that those two might be related. How about all the other women Richard may have assaulted? After all, I heard how Grandpa was hitting on women and not in a nice way, even at his current nursing home. What was he like in his youth? … Shit," Mason muttered. "The old guy was a dirty old man his whole life, it seems."

Markus chuckled. "It comes down to whether we're ready to call this a day or if it'll just be something we still have to keep an eye out for. More offspring out there could mean more to collect on a promise of money later for killing you now."

"That won't make Tesla happy."

"No, it won't. It won't make any of us happy," Markus murmured. "We all want a definitive end to this, so we can feel like it's done and over with. Otherwise we're all in limbo."

Mason muttered, "It never quite works the way we think it should."

"We can still hope. It will be lunchtime soon. Are you okay to eat lunch here?"

Mason mentioned with a dry expression, "As far as I know, I have no dietary restrictions. So, if you want to bring me a nice rare steak, baked potato with all the trimmings, and a shot of bourbon, I won't argue."

Markus gave him a big fat grin. "In that case, just give me a few minutes—minus the whiskey." Then he stepped back out of the room, leaving Mason feeling even more positive about the future.

If only he could get the doctor to sign off on this, he could head home, then really start getting better. There would be something completely different about being at home as opposed to being here as an invalid—something he had never been very good at.

Still, when Markus stepped back in again, he smiled and announced, "Lunch is coming soon."

"Good, I hope it's something decent."

"Oh, it'll be decent," he declared, with a laugh.

Mason grinned at him. "You're enjoying this, aren't you?"

"Hey, it's not a bad thing to see you forced to take a rest like this."

He winced. "Yeah, there is," he argued. "It's terrible and painful as hell."

"I get it," he muttered, "but we are getting somewhere."

"I want to believe you. I do."

"Yet, you don't … not quite," he noted, with a mocking look.

"I do and I don't. I want this to be over with, completely over with."

"Yeah?" Markus gave him a challenging look. "I like the idea of looking for more of Richard's offspring by tracking down the females from Richard's former nursing home and whatever leads can be gained there, but I'm afraid the information will be incredibly unreliable."

"So, how do we find a reliable source? How do get a viable sample pool, so to speak?"

"The only birth records we have any documentation on are the ones that we know about."

"But that would mean we have the mother putting down the father's name, but what about the births that were not attended or where the fathers weren't listed on the birth certificate?"

"That is the concern. I wonder how many of those are out there?"

"I would say a lot, considering the kind of guy Richard is. I'm not sure he was as much of a bastard that way as we think he may be, but I do think that, when it comes to children, he may have spurned some or maybe doesn't even know about others, and that would be a different story."

"If somebody wants something from him, they must provide proof. Even so, I see Richard as the type to investigate regardless, just to confirm."

Mason frowned. "Even proving a blood relation may not be all that simple. DNA testing needs something to compare to. If the parent or the child is not in the DNA database, no connection is there to be found."

"Point taken." Markus considered that. "Though I wonder …"

"Wonder what?" Mason asked, eyeing him intently.

"Just wondering, what would be the incentive?"

Mason suggested, "The old man didn't have a son and really wanted one."

Markus stated, "And we don't know whether his wife had any more children or not. She predeceased him. I'm not sure how long ago."

"We need to find out all that," Mason stated. "Do you want to make some more phone calls?"

"Yeah, I'm on it." Markus stepped back outside the room again. When he returned, a bright smile lit up his face. "We were right to check on his wife, as she had a hysterectomy after the second daughter was born, so she couldn't have any more kids."

"So, that could have started him looking for another sex partner strictly for breeding purposes," Mason pointed out.

"It's certainly possible, not that I particularly like that statement."

"No, and hate it all you like, but I think the old goat would give it a try."

"There's also the chance that *he* wasn't doing very well in that department."

"I would agree with that too. He could have had a dozen kids, unless he just wasn't that fertile himself."

"Do we even know if the two daughters were confirmed to be his?" Markus frowned.

Mason nodded. "And getting proof of that could be pretty challenging. We can't just go around asking for DNA samples on a whim."

"Having a son would be the ultimate victory on Richard's part. Even if he fathered a boy, the old man would have kept that a secret from his wife," Markus pointed out, "right up until he didn't want it to be a secret."

Mason swore at that. "That's very true. Richard could just as easily have made sure that nobody would know until time to read his will."

"And if this secret son—whether it be Steve or twelve other guys—was already getting money from Richard, what was in it for these secret sons to do Richard's dirty work? Like why do anything for this old man, supposedly your father, who never acknowledged you, until now?" Markus pondered that while just looking around, without even seeing the room. "If Steve is Richard's son, does Steve know it? Was Steve also promised an inheritance, like Greg, the grandson? … I would like to talk to him myself."

"You and me both," Mason declared, his tone deepening in fury. "That old bastard put my life on the line, and he didn't give a crap who else he hurt in the process."

"Exactly," Markus agreed. "*Why* is the question that we need to be focusing on. If Richard wanted to take you out, I understand the revenge element. But why wait all this time? This is something Richard could have resolved four years ago, when his grandson Gabe invaded your house and that piece of shit died in the process."

"That's the question, isn't it?" Mason agreed.

"Who the hell knows? Maybe Grandpa Richard thinks revenge is best served cold. I mean, he's going up against the US Navy's finest here. Can somebody that angry wait four years? Has Richard just been biding his time, thinking your guard will be down? But, hell, the sniper was on base, at the base airport no less, where there is bound to be foot traffic, all of the military variety. It seems totally illogical to me to wait, much less to wait to take revenge in an airport on a US Navy base."

"Or just the kind of revenge on a worldwide stage that the old man wanted." Mason shrugged.

Markus sighed. "Right. Maybe he's just that kind of an asshole who's used his money as a carrot to keep his minions under his thumb, doing his beck and call all this time, all for promises of a big payoff in the future, waiting to run across a skilled sniper."

"Make some phone calls," Mason said. "Get Jasper on that secret child theory too."

Markus nodded. "Let me talk to Jasper. I'll have him give you a call." Markus stepped back out again, leaving Mason frustrated and upset that he couldn't just reach out himself. Yeah, Jasper wanted Mason hands-off, at least a little. Mason had to chuckle at that. No way Mason was hands-off now that he was fully conscious. Also no reason he couldn't have a laptop.

He looked over and found Tesla's laptop just sitting there, and he smiled, reaching for it. Just then his cell phone rang. "Jasper," he greeted him in delight.

"Hey, imagine my surprise when I was told to call you."

"Yeah, I'm awake, and that makes all the difference. I'm feeling a ton better, and the doctor's contemplating sending me home, though obviously not to active duty or anything even close. Still, I'll take going home any day over staying at the hospital."

"You're not kidding," Jasper agreed, sounding thrilled. "That is bound to make Tesla's day."

"I think she was more pissed off, thinking I had threatened the doctor or something along that line."

"Did you?" Jasper asked curiously.

Mason laughed. "No. Didn't need to. Surprise, surprise, he thought I was doing just fine."

"And that is the good news." Jasper chuckled. "I just got off the phone from talking with Markus."

"Yeah, I'm just wondering if we've researched the angle of any illegitimate kids, especially knowing Richard's desire to have a son."

"I've spoken to Steve about it. He seems to think nobody else is related just because of the way Richard—his father in his mind—treated him. He also told me how the old man referred to Steve as his secret son, almost like a payback."

"Oh, now that's interesting," Mason noted. "Why would he say that?"

"I don't know, and Steve didn't know anything about how being Richard's son was payback. Steve's already quite pissed off about everything else his father has supposedly done. He appears to be close to Richard, and defensive too."

Mason asked, "How much of being close to his father was because he could do things his grandfather wanted done?"

"That would be my take on it, and, old coots like that, they've always got to be ruling the roost."

"Have you talked to the old man himself about it?" Mason asked Jasper.

"No, I will go talk to him about it now. Every time I get in there, he's even less cooperative."

Mason snorted. "Richard might not be cooperative, but, if he realizes that we now know about Steve and are pushing for more information and asking people about other offspring, Richard might not like the direction we take it."

"Oh, I hear you. I'll go talk to him here in a few minutes, and I'll get back to you." Jasper ended the call.

Mason felt a whole lot better. Following his own lines of inquiry, he quickly started looking into Tesla's notes and realized she had similar searches going. "Damn, Tesla. You're good, aren't you, gal?"

When she responded with a laugh, he looked up in surprise to see her at the doorway, and right behind her was Evan, followed by Markus bringing in a trolley with real food. Mason smelled it a mile away. He sniffed the air and moaned. "Oh my God. I think I've died and gone to heaven."

"And just think," Tesla muttered, with a wry look in his direction, "I had a tuna sandwich."

He stared at her with surprise and pointed. "I'll share."

"No, no, no," she said, with a wave of her hand, "you need to eat. Just the fact that you organized this says an awful lot about the mental condition you're in."

"While lots of swelling caused other issues, the doc didn't find any actual damage to my brain," he shared, "so I'm thankful for that."

"You're not kidding, and, if you can organize something like this meal from your bed"—she shook her head—"obviously you're doing much better."

"I've been telling you that," he reminded her, with a bright smile. "I've been telling you that the whole time. Now I just need to go home."

"And you will," she agreed, "but not until you're cleared."

He cut into the steak, and the taste and the aroma just blew him away. He sat here, chewing slowly, absolutely loving every bite, while the men looked on, grinning. "I had no idea how much real food made a difference." He looked like a kid in a candy store.

"It makes a huge difference," Evan noted, "and, as long as your stomach can handle it, you're fine."

"That would be the test, wouldn't it?" Mason asked, taking another bite. "I'm already thinking about round two."

Tesla snorted at that. "First off, you need to digest round one and see if your stomach doesn't have a conniption fit over your food choices."

"My stomach will be just fine," he declared, with a grin. "Have you ever known it to be anything else?"

"No, but that doesn't mean it won't throw up some barrier and cause quite the stomachache down the road. You did just wake up from a coma, you know?"

"If there's trouble down the road, we'll deal with it then," he said. "At the moment, this food is way too good to even argue about." He motioned at her laptop. "What were you researching?"

She shrugged. "It's probably not of any value, but it occurred to me that anybody with so much pride in family was probably disappointed that he didn't have more children. It wouldn't be surprising that a man of that generation would be disappointed by having only two children, daughters at that. What I was setting up a search for," she explained, as she took up the laptop where it rested at the side of his bed, "was proof of illegitimate children, potentially proof of his own children."

"What do you mean?" Mason asked, between bites.

Both Evan and Markus looked at her in surprise.

She shrugged. "Being pregnant, it tends to be a topic on my mind, but one of the things I was checking out was whether the two daughters were his or not."

At that, Mason whistled silently. "Now that would make sense, particularly if he's changed his will or done anything along those lines."

"I don't even know what may have changed in the will," Tesla replied, "but I can tell you that, based on the two daughters' blood tests, Richard is not their biological father."

CHAPTER 4

TESLA HADN'T MEANT the news to be quite so stupefying. Yet the men all just stared at her in shock. She shrugged. "It's just the way genetics works," she murmured. "So, Richard's not the father to them, but that's a presumed result when he was married to their mother. So we need to verify it with a DNA comparison of all three," she suggested, "but there is no doubt. I did look up Steve's medical records, and it is possible he could be a blood relative. DNA would be required to tell us for sure."

Mason frowned. "So, the old man's wife stepped out on him and passes off her two daughters as if they were his? He may not have been capable of giving her a child, so she steps out and makes it happen, but they still don't get the son he wants. After birthing two girls, the wife's no longer capable of having children, and—"

"So, what then? Richard finds somebody to have a child with?" Markus asked.

"I think so, yes," Tesla said, with a nod.

"Who is it?"

She pointed at her screen. "Cristal." Evan stepped up behind her, looked over her shoulder, and nodded, now writing down her name and address.

"I don't know who she is other than I have a name," Tesla began. "Give me more time, and I can run a full background on her, in terms of whether she's got a criminal record or anything like that. I haven't gotten that far."

"No, but you also got a whole lot further than I expected, and I was just about to embark on that pathway," Markus stated, eyeing her with respect.

She smiled. "Remember? This is the stuff I do."

"I do remember." Markus turned to Mason. "I think he forgot."

"I didn't forget," Mason stated, with an eye roll, "but I was trying to keep her out of it."

"Yeah, well, too bad. We've been pulling on her this whole time."

Evan called Jasper, then quickly relayed the information Tesla had.

"Right," Jasper confirmed, now on Speakerphone. "I'll go visit with this woman."

Evan stated, "I'm coming with you."

"You're sure?" Jasper asked.

"Hell yes," he declared. "I'm not certain what is going on here, but, if we can bring this to a close or at least get some answers, I'm there every time."

"Okay," Jasper replied. "Do you want to meet at the address?"

"Yeah, sounds good." As they ended the call, Evan turned to Tesla and asked, "You're staying here, right?"

"Yes, I'm staying here," she said, with a smile.

Evan looked over at Markus. "You're good if I head out?"

"I'm good." Markus nodded. "Keep in touch. We all want to know where this goes."

And, with that, Evan quickly stepped away.

Markus looked over at the two of them. "I'll be outside." He stepped out himself.

Mason asked Tesla, "Are you sure you're okay?"

"Of course I'm doing okay." She smiled. "I had a shower, did some laundry, and life is good. Best of all, there's a good chance you're coming home soon." She gave a deep sigh and added, "Life is even better than good."

"I'm right there with you on that one," he muttered, as he worked through the massive plate of food.

"The fact that you're eating is pretty amazing," she noted, leaving it at that and staring at him.

"I know, and it means I'm on the mend," he stated, sending a bright grin in her direction. "I just need to ensure the healing continues. So after another day or two in the hospital, we'll be home."

He spoke it with such surety that she believed him. "That is the one thing about you that I've never really understood but have always appreciated," she muttered.

"What?"

"That complete and utter belief in what you are doing."

"Always, because anything less than that, and you're not getting the full value of who you are or the full results of what it is you're here to do." He took another bite, then finally continued. "I know what I'm here to do in life," he declared, with a wry smile. "I'm just blessed that I get to spend it with you."

AS EVAN QUICKLY stepped out of the room, Markus was on his tail.

Markus asked, "Are you good?"

"Yeah, I'm good." He waved a hand about. "Still, I think Janelle and Tesla are right. I don't think this is totally over. You keep an eye on them, will you?"

"Damn right," he declared. "Don't you worry about them. You go see what you can find out, and I'll make sure that nothing happens here."

And, with that assurance, since no killer was better than Markus, Evan headed out to the parking lot. He looked up the GPS directions he had for Cristal's address and drove away. As he pulled up at the nearby address, he found Jasper pulling up right behind him. He smiled as he greeted him. "Amazing that we've come this far, yet we're still not sure."

"It's the *not sure* part that gets me," Jasper confirmed. "I'm sure, but I'm not sure—if you know what I mean."

"I know exactly what you mean, and that's the part that worries me. When the hell do we know for sure?"

"When we run out of bad guys," Jasper stated, with a laugh, "which is already taking way more time to sort through than we thought."

"You've got that right." Evan gave him a begrudging smile. They turned together to look at the house. "It doesn't speak of money. It's got an innocuous look to it really. It's just a house."

It was a typical older plantation style, with a big veranda around the front, but it was showing some age, revealing a lack of care and maintenance. The paint was peeling. The railings needed to be replaced in spots, and Evan wouldn't doubt that the floorboards were likely in equally poor shape.

Walking casually, knowing that likely a neighbor or somebody was keeping tabs on the place, they walked up to the front door and knocked. Evan turned to look around.

"No vehicles anywhere around here," he noted. "The place looks deserted, may have been deserted for quite a while."

"Yeah, it looks that way, but looks can be deceiving," Jasper pointed out. "We can't take that chance."

"No, I get it. It's just frustrating if this is a dead-end lead." Evan waited, and, when he got no answer, he tried again, and again nothing. As they stood here, someone across the street called out to them. Evan turned to see an older woman standing there, a curious look on her face.

She told them, "Nobody's lived there for quite a while."

Evan walked down the front steps to talk to her. "Do you know when the last person was here?"

"Months ago maybe," she said, with a frown. "Or who knows? At least a few weeks."

Knowing there was a big difference between a few weeks and a few months, Evan just waited for her to fill in the information.

Then she sighed and added, "Honestly, I'm not very good with time, but it's been a while."

"Do you know who used to live here?"

"Sure, that woman," she said. She snapped her fingers several times, as if to pull out the woman's name.

Evan asked, with a smile, "Cristal Mark?"

She nodded. "Yes, yes, but then of course you know that, since you're here knocking on the door."

"We were hoping to find her."

"Not sure you will find her here. She was normally around. Then a couple weeks ago she told me how she had to leave. Things were getting dicey."

"Any idea what she meant by dicey?"

"Oh no, I don't think she even knew what she meant. She was quite worried and packed up several bags, then put them in her vehicle," the neighbor lady explained, turning to look at the road.

"Do you know what kind of vehicle she has?"

The woman turned and looked at them suspiciously. "You're not here to hurt her, are you?"

"No, not at all." Evan looked at Jasper and then back at her. "We're also not sure if she's aware that her son's been picked up and is down at the MP station."

She stared at them. "Why would he be picked up? He's an investigator," she stated, then gave them a once-over. "If anything, he should be picking up the bad guys."

"I hear you on that, … and nobody was more surprised than us."

"Is that what you're here for, to pick her up?"

"No, we were here to let her know and to see if she wanted to come down and see him."

"That would be nice," the neighbor lady said, with a look of worry.

Clearly she was hiding information on some drama right under the surface. Evan added, "I'm sure this trouble has been more of a shock to her than anything. So did all this happen a few weeks ago or was it more recent than that?"

The lady shrugged. "Honestly, I don't remember. … It was a couple Saturdays ago, I think." Then she looked around and frowned. "She used to be friendlier. At some point she was less so, more standoffish."

"Any idea why?"

"I don't know." She settled one hand on her hip to try and stand straight. "Something about hoping to come into some big money, but she wasn't sure if it would work out that way."

Evan stiffened slightly at that. "Did she say where from?"

"Something about child support she never got."

"Ah, that makes sense," he muttered, with a nod, "because she never got child support for her son."

The other woman nodded. "Yeah, something like that. I know she was bitter about it, but then I don't know whether she was ever in contact with the father or not. However, she started to change a little bit ago."

"Do you think her son knew about it?"

"Oh, yeah, I think he was part of it—or at least knew something about it." The lady shrugged. "But I don't have details about it, as nobody talked to me about it."

And yet somehow the woman appeared to be a fount of information. "Has she been good friends with anybody in this area?" Evan asked.

"No, not for a while. She worked at an old folks' home for a long time, but she just changed jobs here recently."

Evan stared at her, an indication of what was to come in the back of his mind. He asked her, "Is she at the hospital now, by any chance?"

"Yeah, exactly. How did you know?" She looked at the house behind him and added, "I guess it makes sense that you're here because of her, but I can't see her ever doing anything wrong."

"Why is that?"

"She's just not that kind of person. If she wanted the child support, she probably could have gone after the father of her child a long time ago, but she didn't really want to. I think she was a little afraid, you know? Having a child out of wedlock was hard on her, and she made up all kinds of stories way back when. Yet I've known her for a long time, and, at one point, she told me how her boy was conceived in, … well, not the best circumstances," she whispered. She looked like she was having the conversation of her life. "I took that to mean maybe she was raped or something along that line, but who knows?"

"She mentioned it?"

"*Nah*, she never came out and used that word for it. She just told me that she didn't have a choice." The two men stared at her steadily, and she frowned. "She's had a rough life, so anything she's got coming to her in a good way, I'm all for," she declared, with sympathy in her tone. "Cristal's a good person. So I hope you guys don't mess up anything for her."

"We didn't come to mess up anything," Evan stated, "but her son's down at the station."

"I just can't see that. Something's got to be wrong. All she ever talked about was how good her son was, about all the things that he did, and about how proud of him she was."

"Do you think anything would change her mind about him?"

"No, not at all." The lady laughed. "You've got to understand that a lot of mothers are like that. They're blind right to the bitter end. So, even if her son did do something wrong, it would take a lot for Cristal to believe it."

"What if a lot of money was involved that she thought was hers?"

"I'm not sure, but I would suspect that she would do a lot to get it. She's not in the best of health and won't continue working much longer. I know that was an issue."

"Is she a nurse?"

"She's one of those health care aides, not a nurse, but I don't know what you call them." She gave a wave of her hand, her expression vague. "She worked in some retirement home, looking after people."

"Right," Evan said, noting she was repeating herself. "Do you know about the father? Is there a chance that the father of her child might have been in the nursing home?"

She stopped, and then her face cleared of puzzlement. "I think she did say something about that, like she was surprised to find him there, but it was different now because he was old and broken down."

"Right." Evan nodded. "It's hard to have the same hate for somebody who is clearly heading toward their final days."

"I don't know. I think she would have found the hate just fine." The neighbor lady laughed. "He wasn't a very nice man. She did mention one time that he was wealthy, so maybe that was the whole point. Maybe if he was nearing the end of his life and wealthy, now Cristal is thinking she could get a piece of that for herself."

"That's a possibility."

"She wanted it for herself, but she also wanted it for her son," she added. "He'd suffered a lot growing up because he didn't have his dad."

"Would she ever do anything illegal to get that money?"

"No, not at all—unless it was to help her son," she stated suddenly.

Evan shared a knowing look with Jasper. Evan nodded. "Right, we're back to that *mother* thing."

"Unless you have kids of your own, I don't expect you to understand," the old woman said, staring at him.

"I don't have kids yet," he admitted, with a smile, "but I'm hoping."

Her smile burst free at that. "That's good. Nothing quite like being a parent. It changes you, so, in her case, I don't know. There would have to be strong motivation, but she can't keep working much longer. I know she needed some medical treatment."

"Did she ever ask the father of her child for help?"

"If she did, he probably just would have laughed at her," she replied. "He's not a nice man."

"You know who he is?"

She just waved around her hand at that. "I used to know his name at one time, or at least his first name, but I don't remember it anymore."

"Right." Evan smiled at her. "Thank you for your help."

She nodded. "I hope Cristal's okay." The lady turned to face the house. "As you can see, she hasn't had any money for the upkeep and all."

"Is it hers?"

"I think so, but I think her son had to help pay for it." They all turned to study the house that seemed even more dilapidated by the minute.

Evan asked, "But, if her son was doing fine, and he was an investigator, how come he wasn't helping her more with the house?"

The neighbor lady nodded. "I think that's one of those questions parents frequently have to ask themselves. They did so much for their child but now? How come the child isn't doing much for them?" She slowly turned and started to walk away, then stopped to pivot back to them. "If you see her, say hi for me, will you?"

"We will," Evan assured her. "What's your name?"

"I'm Becky. Becky Smith." And, with that, she slowly meandered down the sidewalk.

Evan looked over at Jasper. "What do you think of that?"

"I think it's interesting," he muttered. "You do have to

wonder why the house is in such rough shape."

"Unless she wanted everybody to assume her financial condition was this way, even if it wasn't necessarily, or if she now has hopes of changing it. Who knows? Maybe this house won't get any love and attention even then."

They turned and looked at the house with a more practiced eye, and Evan murmured, "It will take an awful lot of money to fix it up."

"I was just thinking that," Jasper agreed. "It might be better for them to just walk away."

"They could sell it in as-is condition or put some money back into it to get a better sales price. However, they would need some spare money to do that."

"He's been off for the last few months," Jasper noted, turning to look at Evan.

"Do we know why?" Evan asked.

"He's on medical leave, but I don't know exactly why. It's not in the files."

Evan contemplated that for a long moment. "I wonder how much time it took to set this up and whether he took off work just so he wouldn't be part of the suspect pool."

"I wouldn't be at all surprised," Jasper replied. "If you think about it, that's not a bad way to get out of work and to still be accessible to our ongoing investigations. Medical leave does not require him to terminate his various access privileges."

"Which is another thing that concerns me," Evan shared. "We're assuming Cristal's more or less an innocent victim in all of this, but do we know that for sure?"

"No, we sure don't," Jasper confirmed cheerfully, "and now the problem is, we must track her down, and I highly doubt her son will give us that information."

"He may also have moved her out so she didn't have any idea about what was going on. Maybe he just told her that he would come get her when it was all over with."

"Again, too many questions and no answers."

"So, if she was calling her own shots, where would she go, and would she tell her son?"

"I don't think it would matter if she told her son or not. Even if she told Steve, I don't think he will tell us."

CHAPTER 5

TESLA WOKE TO her phone ringing. She answered it, still groggy. "Hello."

"Hey," Evan asked, "did I wake you?"

"That's all right," she murmured. "I'm always either asleep or on my way in or out of sleep these days. Besides, I would rather you woke me than him."

"That's what I will ask next. Is Mason awake?"

"He's sleeping," she announced, looking over at her husband. "What's up?"

"The woman we went to see, Cristal Mark, left her house what looks like a few weeks ago, packed up her vehicle, and took off. According to her neighbor, Becky—the nosy type, who has a ton of information to share for someone who knows absolutely nothing—Cristal was in a bit of a hurry, and somewhere along the line had mentioned that she was hoping a lot of money was coming her way." He quickly relayed the rest of the information.

Tesla replied, "That sounds like the mother of Steve then. That's for sure. And, from what we know of Richard, he probably did rape Cristal. So we have Steve's mother and father. Just confirm that she worked at the same nursing home as Richard was at before, and I think we've got this paternity issue solved."

"Yeah, it is, but the question now is, where has Cristal gone, and why?" Evan asked.

"She's not a nurse, but has some caregiver-type job."

"Okay, so what is she specifically? Do you know?" At Tesla's silence, Evan continued. "She supposedly has a job at the hospital, more or less a caretaker of some kind. She may be deemed an independent contractor or whatever. We've got calls in to the hospital right now to see if she's on staff or maybe she's taken a leave of absence, like her son did."

"In other words, Cristal could be here," Tesla muttered, stiffening as she looked around.

"It's possible, but it's also possible that she is not involved at all and that her son urged her to get out of town for a vacation or something. We don't know what Steve may or may not have told her to get her out of the way."

"Does he care about her, or is he just using her like apparently other people have used her?" Tesla asked.

"Again, good question." Evan sighed. "What we don't know is the motive behind all this. We will go talk to Steve, but I highly suspect he won't say very much, since it's his mother we're talking about."

"Exactly, yet he's not getting out of jail, so he might do something in order to save his own ass or to make things a little easier. Still, since it's his mother, I doubt he would throw her under the bus."

"Have Mason call me back when he's awake."

"Will do."

After the phone call, she sat up and made her way to the bathroom, wincing at the pain in her lower back just from the movement. She rubbed her belly and whispered to her baby, "This will be over soon, sweetie. Just hold on a little longer. We'll get you there."

When she made her way back out of the bathroom, she walked over to Mason, who was awake now, and smiled at him. "Evan called earlier, so I took it. Now you get to call him back."

He held up his hand for the phone and punched the most recent call, putting it on speaker. "What did you hear?" he asked, and she watched as Evan apparently reiterated everything that they'd just found out. Mason rubbed his face with his free hand. "I think Cristal's probably on the run."

"So, what does that mean?" Evan asked.

"It means this just got dragged out again. She knows her son is in trouble, maybe knew ahead of time, and now we won't find her." He frowned, as he looked over at Tesla. "We can check bank accounts and everything else along those lines to see if there's any money trail of her. Or maybe she's still showing up for work, and that will keep her somewhere close by. Regardless I agree with you. If Richard raped Cristal, conceiving Steve, Cristal may hate Richard but would probably do anything he asked for a big payout that would help her and Steve."

"Exactly. We're on her trail right now," Evan noted. "Jasper is checking into it. I will send you a picture of her, so if you see anybody like that, be on the lookout."

"Sure," he replied. "Send it to Markus too."

"Already done," Evan said cheerfully and disconnected.

Mason turned to Tesla as he handed the phone back. "It makes sense that Cristal would take off."

"Only if she knows everything that's going on," Tesla pointed out. "However, if she's clueless, then this is just about the two of them against this world. Chances are, though, she knows something's going on."

"But did she know about the relationship between Steve and his father?" Mason asked.

"That's the thing that I don't know. Yet, if she's expecting to come into a bunch of money, you would think she knew Steve and Richard were talking and visiting. Maybe if that had something to do with all the things that her son missed out on, it makes even more sense for the son to get to know his father."

Tesla frowned, shaking her head. "It still doesn't make any sense why Cristal would come after you now, as the final attempt on your life or to barter your life for whatever. It's not as if you have the USB keys people are still looking for or you can get the money for her, unless the old man is still pulling strings and will give her the money if everybody else fails. How desperate is Cristal though?"

"It depends," Mason replied. "Seems her house is in rough shape, and she pulled out quickly so she could distance herself. Or she's just not around her home and thinks that would make her hard to find."

"Which it won't, it'll just push back things a little bit, especially given the fact that she's hardly an experienced criminal."

"Yet," Mason argued, rubbing his chin, "we don't know that. Maybe that's what got *Mommie and Daddy* together in the first place."

Tesla's eyebrows shot up at that, and she nodded thoughtfully. "Let me do some digging."

He chuckled. "Is there anything you prefer more than sorting through all this data?"

"In this case, I have a very personal and a very valid interest in keeping you safe," she stated, with a smile. "So let me take a look and see what I can come up with."

She waddled over to her bed and hitched herself up so that she was leaning against the wall, with the laptop on her belly. When she heard a quiet chuckle beside her, she looked over and frowned. "What's so funny?"

"You. Do you see how high up the laptop is?"

"Yeah," she snapped, glaring at him, "I'm very aware. It's not very nice of you to point it out."

"Oh, but I love it. I love how ripe and full you are with my child."

She rolled her eyes at that. "Now you're sounding down-right possessive."

"I have every right to be possessive," he stated, with that smile that still makes her heart melt. "It's my child, but look at where we're at."

"I know," she muttered. "Look at where we're at, but it's not as if we can do anything. I'm pregnant. Remember?"

"Does that stop us from doing anything?" he asked, with a questioning look in her direction. "I wasn't thinking it would, and apparently it doesn't."

She glared at him. "You're not allowed to think about it anyway."

"Ah, but we already mentioned that I was going home in a few days," he reminded her, waggling his eyebrows.

She burst out laughing. "I do not understand how such a heavily pregnant woman could turn you on."

"That's because you are *my* heavily pregnant woman, of course," he explained, with a smile. "I don't think there could ever be a point in time when you wouldn't turn me on," he stated, staring at her. "I don't care if you're wearing a potato sack, if you're heavily pregnant, or if you're old and gray." He gave her a coy smile, "You're still the woman I love."

She sighed at the emotions in his tone and said, "You will get me crying again if you don't stop."

He winked at her. "I love you even when you're crying."

She groaned. "Knock it off, please." She turned her attention back to her computer. "Okay." She sighed and looked at the screen. "I find no other property coming up in either Steve's name or Cristal's."

"He wouldn't have lived in that apartment with her, would he?"

"In that house, you mean? I don't think so. Apparently it wasn't in very good shape."

"He was making good money, but I don't know what his other financial commitments would be. There's a chance— does Steve have any kids?"

She went to typing quickly. "I don't know. Let me find out." It didn't take very long, and she announced, "I don't see a birth certificate with Steve listed as the father, but he had a fairly long-term relationship, based on my search of social media accounts."

"That's interesting, so if they had any kids—"

"That would be an entire family line that old man Richard either doesn't know about or just recently discovered."

"If it's a relative of Steve's, then Richard probably knows."

"And that's likely why he has that whole family thing on the go again."

"That's possible, but maybe they have to prove themselves first," Mason suggested. "It's not likely the old man will change at this stage."

"They do sometimes," Tesla noted, looking over at him. "I get that the chances of it aren't very good with Richard, but it does happen. Aren't they both in custody, Richard and

Steve, right? Can't somebody go talk to them?"

"Sure." Mason smiled. "We can talk until we're blue in the face, but, if the prisoners don't want to talk back, you know how that will go."

"But now that people know something about Richard's other family, that just might change things."

He nodded. "I'll send Jasper a text about it." Just then Jasper phoned him.

"Hey, Mason. We're on the way to talk to the father and son. We'll see what they have to say about Cristal's whereabouts, among other things."

"Good, and apparently there's a chance that the old man might have another grandchild too, by Steve."

"Shit. Did Tesla find that?"

"Yes, though she's still confirming. Although the couple weren't married, they were apparently together for many years. Based on a change of residence, they broke up about the time she got pregnant. No father is noted on the birth certificate, but there is still a chance her baby is his."

"So, either he didn't want it or it's somebody else's, and that was the reason for the breakup?"

"Any of that and more is possible."

"How long ago?"

"Looks like about eighteen years."

"Great," Jasper noted. "I wouldn't even put it past old man Richard to be involved in that too."

"I would hope not," Mason said, with a groan. "That would just be so wrong."

"Everything this old guy does is wrong, but we'll see if we can get some more answers." And, with that, he disconnected.

Mason looked over at Tesla, frowning, as he put the

phone on the bedside table. "You heard all that?"

"Yeah, I did." She took a deep breath. "I don't even want to think that could be what happened, as that would be just so wrong."

"Even if Steve didn't want a child, that might have been enough to change things with his longtime girlfriend."

"Yeah, but Steve's own father, if it proves to be Richard per DNA tests, also left Steve at birth. How could Steve do that to his child too?" Tesla shook her head. "Yet it's hard to say what each person does in those situations. People have very different reactions when they find out they are pregnant."

Mason smiled. "In my case I was delighted, … both times."

"But we were also married, in an established healthy relationship, and we were ready," she stated, deep in thought. "That doesn't mean Steve was ready for fatherhood and its responsibilities. For all we know, he hated his father for never acknowledging him or his mother for never telling him who his father was. Meaning, Steve may have father issues that he wouldn't want to pass on to his own child, yet still carries on that stigma by being the absent father himself."

"And yet Steve's girlfriend had a baby eighteen years ago. That's been quite a few years ago," he pointed out. "Maybe Steve wanted to know his child at some point in the past."

"It could happen, so it's anybody's guess. However, chances are, Steve just didn't want anything to do with a baby—or didn't know about the baby. I wonder if Cristal knew about the girlfriend being pregnant because, if Steve left his own child, the way Richard left Steve …" Tesla left that thought hanging.

"That could cause quite a problem, couldn't it?"

"But Cristal would also want proof that it was her grandchild. Otherwise I'm not sure she would take it on. She had already been a single mother once with no paternal support, and back then she would potentially be a single grandparent taking on a child all by herself again—or taking in both mother and child. Plus, Cristal's home revealed a lot about her financial status. Obviously Cristal was struggling to support herself. The tangled webs we weave," Tesla murmured.

Mason smiled at her. "Very much so, but, on the other hand, with a little bit of time and practice, these tangled webs do tend to unravel."

She chuckled. "As long as they unravel soon enough," she muttered and then went back to her research.

When she looked over at Mason a little later, he had fallen back asleep. She smiled and whispered, "Good, that's what you need. Your body *and mind* need rest, not the stress and distraction of this mess."

Tesla hated that he was even involved to the extent that he was, which meant his brain would never shut down, since he wasn't willing to give up taking point on so many matters. She continued to watch over him, while doing as much research as she could. Still, she didn't come up with anything new.

Needing another nap herself, she curled up in bed, and closed her eyes, with a final whisper to Mason, "This will all be over soon."

JASPER AND EVAN walked into the interview room, where old man Richard sat.

"I will be dead before I give you any information," he stated, with a cackle.

"Yeah, I would imagine so," Jasper agreed, with a smile. "Obviously we know about your son, Steve. Now the next question is whether you know about your grandchild from that wing of the family?"

The old man stiffened.

"I just wonder how much of all this you've been manipulating behind everybody's back."

"I guess you'll never know," he jeered, with a small smile. "You can guess all you want, but it won't give you any answers."

"How much of all this is just revenge? If Gabe was killed and wasn't even your blood grandson, why do all this?"

"Because he *was* my grandson," he sneered, "and nobody does that to my family."

"Gabe wasn't your grandson by blood because his mother wasn't your daughter by blood. Neither of your daughters have your blood."

Richard glared at him. "Gabe *was* my grandson, and I'm not listening to any of those lies."

Jasper and Evan now stood and moved into the separate interview room with Steve.

He looked up and sneered. "What are you guys investigating anyway?" he asked, with a laugh. "Jeez, I would have had this case in the bag a long time ago."

"Interesting," Jasper noted. "So, do you have any relationship with your child?"

Steve stiffened and glared at him. "I don't have a son, but nice volley. You lure me into thinking that we will have a nice conversation and then hit me with something stupid like that? Of course it won't work. You think I haven't spent a lifetime learning those same techniques and using them on other people?"

"Of course you have," Evan stated, giving him a hard glance. "You've done all kinds of shit for people, right? Particularly the old man?"

"Yeah, well, I have a reason for that too."

"Of course there was, and the reason isn't necessarily one that works in your favor."

"Doesn't matter if it does or not," he declared, sending another sneer their way. "You guys are just full of shit if you think I will talk to you about anything."

"Oh, you might talk to us eventually. I'm not sure we'll give a shit enough to wait for it though."

"I won't speak to the likes of you," he stated, with a laugh. "You guys must be getting shit from the brass for taking so long. Some elite investigators you are, aren't you?"

Jasper smiled at Steve's attempts to rile him. "Doesn't matter what kind of wonderful investigator I am," Jasper said cheerfully, "because all you will be from now on is a felon, spending the rest of your life in prison. That's something noteworthy."

"No, I won't spend the rest of my life in jail. I'll be a model prisoner, and I'll be sure to get reformed and to get therapy. Then I can tell them all about my devastating childhood and how it affected me—that need to bond with my father and all that *blah, blah, blah*. I'll think of something," he vowed, with a smile. "I'll be out of the slammer in no time."

"You think so, *huh*?"

"I know so, Mr. Elite." He stared at Jasper intently. "We've heard it time and time again, how every felon who shouldn't be out is out, and the ones who went in for absolutely nothing other than a minor possession deal are still stuck in there." When Jasper remained silent, Steve smiled. "Do you think I haven't got it all worked out? I won't do anything to jeopardize my case."

"What about your mother?"

"What about my mother?" he snapped. "You keep her out of this."

"Cristal's missing."

"Good," he declared, with a nod. "I told her to get out of town, but she insisted on finishing her shifts because she was needed at the hospital. Plus, I needed her at the hospital to keep tabs on the people I needed information on," Steve shared, with a shrug. "Now, with that over with, she should have booked it. I'm glad to hear she finally did."

"What about that house of hers, the one that's falling apart?" Jasper asked.

"What about it?" Steve waved a hand. "She wouldn't stay long-term anyway."

"It sure looks like you could have done more for her over the years."

"Sure, looks like it, doesn't it?" He snorted. "That's just another tactic for you guys to make me feel bad about my mother," he replied, with a mocking smile.

"I guess she probably didn't appreciate your relationship with the old man."

Steve shrugged. "She came to understand it at the end."

"Or she was just hoping she would finally get all that money that Richard should have helped her out with over the years."

"She was probably thinking something like that," he agreed, "and I would have made sure she was taken care of. However, you guys have messed that up for her. If she wanted to get some revenge on the old bastard, I wouldn't be against it."

Jasper frowned at Steve. "You would like to see your mother go to jail for something like this?"

"Why not? If it got me out of here, I would take it."

"What would she do, break you out?" he asked, with a note of amusement.

At that, Steve smiled. "You don't get anything, do you?"

"No, I sure don't. Yet you won't get any of Richard's money that you think is still stashed away either."

"It *is* stashed away, and it will be in my name. So I'll have it by the time I do my stint in prison and become a reformed citizen," he explained in a mocking tone. "I've waited a long time for all that money, so waiting a little bit longer won't make any difference."

Jasper asked Evan, "Should we play the recording we have of Richard?"

"What about it?" Steve asked.

"Richard states he has no money left."

"Good one. I wouldn't believe that con even if you had a recording in what sounded like Richard's words."

"We tried to tell you. Just remember that. What about Greg, his grandson?"

"He's in jail too, and for some serious shit. I doubt he's got the chops to make it through what's coming to him while incarcerated, not without causing more trouble,"

"He's not happy at all to find out he's not getting all that money that was supposed to come to him. And now you seem to think it will go to you."

"It is coming to me," Steve claimed. "I made sure to get the old man to sign some paperwork so he didn't try and screw me out of it."

"You don't think he screwed you out of it anyway?"

"I've got the paperwork," Steve confirmed, with a wry smile, "so it doesn't matter."

"Yet paperwork can be changed, particularly if you're a felon."

"Not something like this," he stated. "I had lawyers draw it up."

"Lawyers who knew exactly what you were doing?" Jasper asked.

"No, of course not." Steve shook his head as he looked up at Jasper. "I'm not such a fool as to end up without insurance in all this."

"Sure, but what about if dear old dad made it a condition that you succeed in the job, and then and only then will the money come to you."

"There was a condition that I succeed, but the condition was just for the extra money. Regardless he owes me for the rest of it anyway."

"Did you collect already?" Jasper asked.

He just smiled and didn't say anything.

Evan noted, "Good thing we know that now. We'll have to go get that money too."

"Go ahead, try and find it." Steve smiled.

"Will your mother have access to it, at least when you get killed in jail?" Evan asked.

"I won't get killed in jail," he declared. "I haven't done anything that will get me put anywhere but into a minimum-security penitentiary." Steve laughed. "I'll be out in no time."

Jasper and Evan exchanged a glance, knowing it was all too possible—unless they could nail him for a lot more.

Evan listened as Jasper questioned Steve a few more

minutes. Then Evan decided to go another direction. "What about your own child?"

He stiffened. "I don't have anything to do with any supposed child, if it's even mine," he shared, with a sneer.

"So, you were okay doing the same thing to the mother of your child, as the old man did to Cristal? Doing the same thing to your kid that Richard did to you?"

Steve shrugged. "I don't know what the hell Cristal was even thinking about when getting involved with Richard," he muttered. "If she thought he would save her from her life of servitude, she was wrong."

"Guys like that never make for good parents," Evan noted, with a smile. "You don't hold it against him?"

"I did as I was growing up, but not afterward, not once I understood."

"Oh, you mean, once your girlfriend got pregnant with your child, and you decided to ditch both of them?"

"I didn't promise her anything, so no way I would get hooked up and tied down with her. I wanted something different in my life, not to spend every moment working like a dog to pay bills," he declared, with a shrug. "The single life suited me much better."

"And what about your child?"

"Doesn't matter about my supposed child," he stated, glaring. "Why do you keep harping on that?"

"I wonder why a guy like you, who had a rough childhood because of no money, would put your own kid in the same situation?"

"Tough luck," he said, with a snort.

"Like your life," Evan said, staring at him.

"Yeah. Don't I know it. I told you that I wasn't getting tied down."

"What about your mother having a relationship with her grandchild?"

"Nope, I insisted that she didn't," Steve snapped. "She might cross me on some things, but they're only minor things. She would never cross me on that."

"Ah, and what about your father?"

"Nope, Richard doesn't know."

"*Ha.* You think Cristal didn't tell Richard?"

"There would be no reason for her to tell him. And, if she had, the old man would have mentioned something to me."

"Yeah, he probably would have patted you on the shoulder, and you could have just shared a laugh, right? *Stupid women* and all that."

"Yeah, something like that." Steve smiled. "You make it sound like I'm different from any other guy," he pointed out. "I'm not different. None of us want to get caught with a pregnancy like that."

"And yet you were there for creating the child."

"I don't give a shit," he said, with a sneer. "Besides, I don't have too many healthy swimmers."

"So, you've got the same health issues as your father?"

"Yeah, apparently," he said, not shying away from the topic, "which is nice in a way because it's pretty hard to get caught, until you get these women who think you're stupid."

"Right, and did you ever get DNA tested?"

"Nope, I sure didn't," he snapped. "I don't want to know."

"Meaning that it wouldn't change anything?"

"Exactly." He appeared bored, as he stared around the room. "I'm through here. I would like to go back and work on my reform," he quipped, with a pious look in their direction. "I know you're all still here, stumbling around in the dark, without a clue as to what's going on, … but that's your problem."

"Oh, I think we have a damn good idea what's going on," Jasper shared, with a knowing smile, "and I think—just like the grandson, Greg—you, Steve, think you've got a bundle coming your way. However, the old man gets the last laugh. He's pulled the wool over your eyes."

"Of course he tried. That's what he does, but that doesn't mean he's succeeding," Steve declared on a laugh. "He doesn't have as much money as I'd hoped he had, but I got what I could already, and the rest is coming to me, once we can get the job finished."

"*If* you get the job finished," Jasper clarified, "but the joke's on Richard because both Greg and Gabe, his *grandsons*, weren't even Richard's blood."

Steve smiled. "You hadn't figured that out yet, had you?"

"Oh, we had, at least it's under discussion," Jasper noted, "but the old man doesn't seem to know or doesn't want to know."

"No, and I will save that for a punch line." Steve cackled. "I just want to see the look on his face when he figures it out."

"But then you don't know for sure."

He shrugged. "That whole shooting blanks thing is a pretty good giveaway."

"Yet he managed to have you."

"Yeah, which is damn funny in the long run, but, just like me, we've got like a one-in-a-million chance of creating a child. Which is also why I know that the one you call my kid … *isn't* my kid." Again Steve laughed.

"And yet, just like your own father, it could very well be your child."

"Too damn bad for it then"—Steve sneered—"because I don't give a shit. And I'm done talking."

When Evan stepped out of the interview room, he phoned Tesla. "Do you have a current address for Steve's old girlfriend?"

"No, I don't, but let me see if I can come up with something. Why?"

"I'm just wondering about something. He says that his mother had no relationship with his girlfriend after they split up or with the supposed grandchild, but I'm thinking Cristal might not have been quite so hard-hearted when it was her own son being a jerk."

"Meaning that she might be there with the jilted ex and the grandchild now?"

"It's possible," Evan said. "Also, if you could get a picture of his mother, that would be great."

"I have an old picture of Cristal," Tesla shared, "or I can get one off the hospital board that might be more current."

"Did you ever figure out where she's working?" Evan asked.

"She took a few days' leave of absence from the hospital," she replied.

"We're also talking to management back at the retirement home where she worked before. Jasper is on that call right now."

"I imagine she was probably an exemplary employee," Tesla suggested. "She wouldn't have risked being let go for failure to do her job. You mentioned how her house was not in great shape, right?"

"Terrible shape from the looks of it, but her son wasn't

particularly bothered about it. Steve had good money coming in from his navy paycheck. Plus, he already got a good chunk of money from Richard already, if we can believe that much from him. Yet I don't think he intended to share any of that with Cristal."

"I can look into that," Tesla offered.

"If you can, we might grab it and freeze those accounts."

"Yeah, that would be nice," she muttered. "I'll work on that and send you the photo I have."

"Don't worry about that. Jasper just got a photo from the hospital."

"Good enough, send it my way too. Plus one of Steve, if you have a current one handy."

"Already done," Evan said cheerfully.

"I'll look at them in a few minutes," Tesla replied, "but also send it to Janelle."

"Right, she thought something was recognizable about somebody there. Jasper, send that photo of Cristal to me too. I'll pass it along to Janelle, plus one of Steve. She couldn't quite figure out who it was who reminded her of Steve. … Okay, I sent those to Janelle too."

GUILLIAM CALLED EVAN a moment later. "That photo of the woman is somebody we're looking out for at the hospital?"

"It's Steve's mother, Cristal," Evan explained. "She's been working at the hospital very recently, after working for decades at the old folks' home where Richard had once been."

"Christ, it makes you wonder how the base is screening

who they hire into the hospital these days."

"I think the staffing shortage is so bad that nobody even cares who they've hired. As long as they show up for work and do the job, they're good to go."

"Sad situation," Guilliam muttered.

"Also I sent you Steven's photo. Plus, we're looking for a photo of the grandchild, who is probably Steve's son. At least we think it is a boy."

"Grandson? Another one?"

"Yeah, you don't know about this one." Evan quickly filled him in on Steve possibly having an illegitimate child of his own. That child would be in his late teens now, with no relationship with his father either.

"Crap." Guilliam snorted.

"I know, and we don't yet know if this is a continuation of the same issue we have with protecting Mason or if he's completely out of it."

"Does Steve's mother even know of this potential grand-child?" Guilliam asked.

"Steve claims that his mother isn't allowed a relationship with any supposed child of his, and Steve made that very clear early on to her."

"Great, so she's got a son who likes to play games, who bosses her around and gives her orders, just like Steve's father—who may or may not have forced himself on her. Chances are, Cristal won't talk either."

"The old man told us how she's simple and uneducated, and he was totally disgusted as he said it."

"Jeez," Guilliam muttered.

"She was an aide or an orderly or whatever at the old folks' home and had been for decades. It's hardly her fault that was the level of education she got, considering the level of poverty she faced."

"She did raise the boy on her own, no thanks to Richard, so Steve and Richard both shouldn't be quite so mocking."

"Yeah, Richard's just that kind of guy," Evan noted. "And Steve, the son, isn't much different. You and I didn't meet Steve earlier when we joined Jasper's team because Steve had been off on medical leave, so not an active part of the original investigative team."

"Do we know what that medical leave was for?" Guilliam asked.

"The file was suspiciously silent on the matter, but we were able to find out that he's got it down as stress and PTSD from some of his cases."

"Crap, something that nobody will touch or will make an issue of. You should talk to Sam and Morgan about it. They both worked with Steve, so they might have more insight than we do on him. Morgan might be looking for a way to be helpful, considering he's in jail and in some hot water."

"Yeah, we've got that on our schedule," Evan said.

Guilliam added, "We're also still trying to get a hold of the old man's last living daughter, who's not his blood. Anyway she was getting cancer treatments out of state and is due back soon."

"I'm sure she'll absolutely love that conversation," Evan muttered, with a sigh.

"Probably not. The only potential good thing from our perspective is, if something is going on, and if she and her sister aren't Richard's children by blood, then it's possible she might want to get some things off her chest, before things continue down this nasty path."

"Right, but that's a long shot too."

"I know. Anyway I'll keep you posted." Then Guilliam was gone.

With that, Evan turned to Jasper, smiled and shared, "Both Sam and Morgan are available to question further about Steve."

"Good, let's go," Jasper agreed. "The sooner we talk to them, and we get a hold of the mother, we'll at least have whatever information is available."

"You think the mother has anything to do with this?"

"Either mother, you mean?"

"I don't see it in this case, but we've certainly seen female killers before."

"I know, and it always blows me away when we get them. It's just the opposite of what we expect."

"I know, and, because of that, it's almost like the females get away with murder." On that note, they turned and made their way back to the office.

When they walked in, Sam sat there, shaking his head. Evan introduced himself.

"What? You will become a new investigator too?" Sam asked with a sneer.

"I'm here to help work the case and won't be on this team. I've already got too many irons in the fire as it is. However, Tesla and Mason are my friends."

"That's nice, but you're not privy to any of this shit," Sam snapped, with his typical bad attitude. "So you don't get to ask me anything."

"That's fine, I'll just sit here and wait while Jasper does. It's not as if you're *not* involved, considering it has to do with your coworker."

"What coworker? I'm not saying shit about Morgan, if that's what you're after."

Jasper pulled a chair around and sat facing him. "Sam, I know you are pissed at the way things went down early on, but your shitty damn attitude didn't help any. So, what do you know about the illness that's had Steve off on medical leave?"

"Nothing. I mean, he could be a little bit erratic at times. I wondered a time or two if he was using. I tried to talk to him about it once, to hook him up with some help, but he told me that he wasn't, that it was some prescription drugs the doctor had put him on but nothing too horrific. What can I say though?"

"In case you don't know, he's already confessed to being involved in a lot of this regarding the sniper shooting of Mason. Steve requested and was granted medical leave for PTSD. He was using that to maintain access to all the cases that he needed to, while working the other side of this investigation, and to stay out of the inevitable awkward situations that working on the investigative team would have put him in."

Sam just stared at him, and he shook his head. "That's just BS."

"Oh, it's BS all right," Jasper agreed, "but Steve's already locked up and confessed to a good share of it, since we caught him red-handed."

"Damn," Sam muttered, scrubbing his face. "I suppose that's what got everybody all riled up in the first place."

"It sure didn't add to the confidence level."

"No, no, it wouldn't," he said, with a sigh, "and I presume you're taking over the team when this is over?"

"I already took over, as you well know," Jasper confirmed, with half a smile.

"Yeah, I heard that earlier," Sam admitted, "but I was

hoping it wouldn't be permanent."

"It is permanent," Jasper stated. "By the way, I was offered the job before I ever got here."

Sam stared at him in surprise.

Jasper nodded. "When Mason was shot, I stepped in on a temporary basis," he explained, "to see who and what I wanted to work with." Sam winced. Jasper smirked, then nodded. "Now, if you want references and the chance to move on to other jobs, you'll be as open with us about the involvement of anybody else in this mess who we can possibly find."

Sam went red in the face at first, but then all the color drained away.

"If you won't be cooperative on all measures," Jasper added, starting again, "you can take a hike and go find a job on your own, but you sure as hell won't be returning to this office for a reference."

Sam just stared at him, then snorted. "So, I guess that's your not so subtle way of saying I don't have a job anymore."

"Yeah, it sure is," Jasper declared, "not that you expected any differently. I can't imagine the brass would even allow it, not after the indiscretions your colleagues made."

"I was hoping I was cleared."

"Understood, but, at this point, it's not me making that decision. Apparently the brass have decided that your friendship with Steve and Morgan has you looking compromised at a level that they aren't willing to accept."

"Crap." Sam groaned. "Yet, if the situations were reversed, I would have probably done the same. However, I don't and never did know about their involvement in Mason's case. I've been good friends with both of them at different times."

Jasper asked, "Since we've already got Steve locked up, and he's talked, what do you think? Is he capable of this?"

He frowned and then nodded. "He's definitely capable," Sam conceded. "There's always been that edge to him. It made him a good investigator."

"It also made him a little more susceptible to blackmail," Jasper noted, looking over at Sam. "I'm sure he will use all kinds of excuses in the upcoming trials, but you've got to realize he's involved in a lot of this."

"That's just unbelievable," Sam muttered, sitting back.

"So, give me your history with Steve, everything that you're willing to share about your relationship, about him, about his family, about his mother."

"His mother? I didn't think he had a mother."

Jasper looked from Sam to Evan and back again. "He has a mother, and he has an illegitimate child."

Sam stared at him, shaking his head. "If that's the case, I apparently don't know shit about Steve."

"That's what we were afraid of. He's basically been keeping a quiet little personal life here versus anything anybody would recognize."

"I would have sworn that his mother was dead. And, in the domestic department, he'd had a long-term relationship, but he broke it off when she cheated on him. So he wouldn't get into that again."

"What if she didn't cheat on him?" Jasper asked. "Would he have been the kind to step up and to give her child support, without being forced by the courts?"

Sam winced at that. "Not sure he would have, although he was pretty vocal about being an only child raised in poverty most of his life. I thought his mother was long gone."

"Steve may well have intentionally given you that impression, but, not only is she not dead, currently she's packed up everything at her house and has gone missing."

Sam stiffened at that.

Jasper nodded. "So, I don't know whether Steve told her to get out, she finally got wind of what was going on, she knew from the beginning, or she has another plan."

Staring at Sam, Evan spoke up. "We're obviously looking for her now."

Sam frowned and turned to Jasper. "Steve would have had access to everything here on the Mason case."

"Precisely. He had access, utilized that access, gave out information, and used his access to confidential files to blackmail people into doing what he thought they needed to do."

"Ah, crap, you're talking about Drew now, aren't you?"

"Yeah, I sure am, and likely Morgan too, although I don't know for sure about the rest who were bribed. It will take some time to sort through it all because so many of the players are dead. We might not ever know."

Sam frowned. "I obviously didn't know Steve all that well. … I know that sounds terrible because we worked with the guy, but he wasn't all that easy to get to know. Steve was the kind of guy where you never knew where you stood with him, but he was good at his job, so it didn't matter."

"*Good at his job* apparently wasn't good enough," Jasper murmured. "So, you have nothing to help us find out where his mother might have gone?"

"No, I don't have anything to suggest," Sam replied. "I know that sounds like I'm not cooperating, but, damn it, none of this makes any sense. Obviously Steve's not the guy we thought he was, but I'm not hiding anything here," Sam claimed.

And, with that, Evan got a call, and he stepped out of the office to take it. It was Tesla.

"I have an address for Steve's ex-girlfriend."

"Good. Where is she at?"

"She works at a bank, where apparently everybody loves her."

"Okay, I'll stop in and have a talk with a few people."

"She's not at work today," Tesla noted, "and hasn't been for a couple days."

"*Uh-oh*," Evan muttered. "Any idea where she is?"

"I do have a home address coming through from the manager. I'll send it to you as soon as I get it. Ooh, I've got a text." He waited, and she told him, "It's coming your way now."

And, with that address in hand, he walked back into the office and motioned at Jasper, who came right over. "We've got a home address for the ex-girlfriend, and she hasn't been at work for the last few days." Jasper stared at him, and Evan nodded. "I suggest we go make a house call."

"Yeah, you're not kidding. I'll drive."

CHAPTER 6

MASON ASKED FROM his hospital bed, "What was that all about?" Tesla quickly filled him in. He repeated that last part. "She works at a bank, but she's not been at work for the last few days?"

"Yeah," she replied.

He groaned. "All these women and nobody gives a crap about them."

"That's what it looks like," Tesla agreed, "but then not as many women have been as lucky as I have been."

He gave her a ghost of a smile. "You would say that," he teased, "because you love me."

"I do say that because I do love you, yes, but I also know the kind of a man you are. Some of these other men, honest to God, I would be okay if they were just taken out back and dumped."

He chuckled. "So fierce," he murmured.

"So many upset lives," she pointed out. "So many are hurting, but, if people would just step up and be honest, you would hope they would help each other." He motioned for her to come over. "Are you okay?" she asked instantly, as she walked closer.

"I'm doing okay," he replied, with a smile. "How about

you?"

"I'm fine," she said, sounding tired. "I really want to be out of here and back home again, but I know that we're coming down to the wire on this whole mess, so I'll take it."

"Absolutely."

Markus poked his head in. "You guys up for food?"

"I'm absolutely up for food," Mason declared, facing him. "You had to ask?"

He chuckled. "Just checking."

"Oh, good, and, yes, food, please."

"Okay, I already ordered it anyway," he said, with a big grin at Mason. "Give it about twenty minutes."

"What did you order?"

"Italian, and lots of it."

"Good. Will you eat with us?"

"*Ha*, I'm on guard duty. Remember?"

"I know what you're saying, but a big guy like you has to eat too."

"We'll see. You can go ahead and eat. Then we'll see if you leave me anything."

"Even saying that means he will, and you know that," Tesla said.

Markus just chuckled and headed out again. At the doorway he stopped, then turned to them with a smile. "Just remember, guys. In a couple more days, you'll be out of here and back home." He closed the door behind him.

Tesla looked over at her husband. "He's right, babe. Just a couple more days and this stage of our life will be over."

"I can't wait." Mason gently covered her hand with his. "What we do need is some time for ourselves, without guards, without anybody."

She chuckled. "For the record, sir, you are in no condition for any hanky-panky," she declared. "So, if that's what you have in mind, forget it."

"Hanky-panky," he repeated, with a silly grin, waggling his eyebrows. "I do love that term, and I especially love it when you talk dirty."

She rolled her eyes at that. "That's hardly talking dirty," she muttered, "but it's not happening regardless."

"It might happen though," he added, as the gleam in his gaze deepened, "if we ever get home."

"We will get home, and it most definitely will happen when you are doing better. However, for now, get some rest before the food comes." She smiled, then returned her attention to her laptop.

When a knock came several minutes later, the door popped opened, and Markus walked in with a trolley.

"Wow, when you deliver food, you deliver food," Mason stated, with a grin.

"Hey, you're a big guy, like me. So you need real food, not hospital food."

"I won't argue with that," Tesla said, with a nod, "but your ability to turn around and get something like this to happen so quickly is quite amazing."

"Hey, I can get all kinds of shit to happen," Markus declared, "and don't you forget it."

"Not forgetting anything," she muttered, "particularly when I see this." She walked over to the bed and helped Mason sit up. With the trolley moved over enough that they could see the spread themselves, she stared in amazement. "Markus, this looks lovely."

"Good, then maybe you'll eat more."

She rolled her eyes at that. "I'm hardly starving."

"You won't get the chance to starve either," he pointed

out. "Now sit down and eat." And, with that, he quickly served them up plates, then enjoyed a plate with them. He bulldozed through his food, then announced, "Eat up. I'm heading back out to the hallway."

"Are you sure? There's still plenty of food here."

He rolled his eyes. "Not for long," he said, with a chuckle. "I will be disappointed in you if you leave some because I'm pretty sure, between the two of you, you're more than capable of polishing off the rest of it. As for me"—he patted his tummy—"I'm pretty good."

"On the other hand," she added, as he walked to the door and opened it, "I'm not likely to—"

Out of nowhere, a stranger hit Markus in the head with the butt of his gun. Markus fell backward, stumbling before collapsing on the floor.

A young man stepped into the room and quickly closed the door behind him. He looked at them and sneered. "Well, well, all those pros out there, and look what I managed to do."

"What you managed to do," Tesla said, "is hurt a friend of ours."

"Yeah, and a guy like that won't be out for long," he noted, as he lifted his handgun, "so I don't have much time. Sorry—"

The door opened again, and a woman called out, "No!"

He turned and stared at her. "We've had this conversation already," he snapped and quickly turned to face Mason.

"Yes, we have," she agreed, "and the answer is still no. You're not doing this."

"Sure I am," he said, with a laugh. "Do you know how much money is at stake?"

"Maybe none," Mason shared. "We've heard so many

people talk about all this money they were committing these crimes for, and yet old man Richard doesn't have much left anymore."

"Yeah, that's what you say," the gunman argued, "but he's loaded, like hundreds of millions."

"No, he's not worth much of anything now," Tesla stated. "He's made some bad decisions, and his son-in-law has made some bad business decisions. There isn't much left now."

"So what? Still tons of money are at stake, and I want my share. I was cheated out of all of it."

"A lot of you feel you were cheated by Richard, but I wonder how much of that cheating is real." Tesla looked at the older woman standing there, trembling, as she tried to stop the young man from following through with this murder. And, sure enough, it was the woman who had been upset at Janelle for going into the nursing station to make tea. Those sketch artists were uncannily accurate. Now side by side with her grandson, the resemblance between the two was unmistakable. Tesla noted that Steve looked like both his mother and his teenage son. "Hi, Cristal. This is your grandson, isn't it?"

The woman gasped, and the grandson turned ugly. "What the hell do you know?"

Mason spoke up. "We know that you're Steve's son and that he dumped your mother because he didn't believe you were his child, or, if he did believe, … he didn't give a crap."

"That's because he didn't give a crap," the son declared. "That's what men like him do."

"So why do you want to become one of them?" Mason asked.

"Who said I was?" he asked, staring at him.

"You're here, and you're ready to kill me," Mason stated, "without any justification, without even knowing what it's all about."

"I tried to tell him," Cristal added, "but he won't listen."

"No, young men like this," Mason noted, "they have a tendency to think with their egos and not with their brains."

The young man glared at him. "You're awfully cocky for a man facing a gun."

"I've faced a lot of guns in my life," Mason declared, "and, yeah, you have a chance right now to ruin my life, to ruin my wife's life, to ruin the life of the child she's carrying. And, if murder is all you're into, what's holding you back?"

"Test me, and you'll find out."

"You are being tested right now. You do realize that if you shoot both of us, then you may have to shoot your grandmother too, a woman who risked a lot to have a relationship with you."

Cristal was shaking and crying and trying to reason with her grandson. "You can't do this. You just can't."

"How did he get in touch with his grandfather?" Mason asked Cristal.

"I made the mistake of telling him about Richard," she whispered. "Over the years he's given me a little bit of money to survive. Not much, never enough," she muttered, "but we made it. And then, when I was working at the home, and he was there, he told me it was too damn bad that I wouldn't have any grandkids because at least they would be my blood. I didn't dare say anything, but I guess my face was an open book, and suddenly he knew. Once he knew, he hassled and bugged me until I told him."

"And, once she told him, Richard reached out to talk to me," the grandson declared, with a smile. "It's always nice to know that everybody in the family tried hard to keep me away from him."

"Maybe because he's a mass murderer," Tesla declared, without hesitation.

"He is not. He's just looking for revenge."

"Revenge?" she repeated. "What is revenge all about? You just turn around and destroy other people's lives?"

"Your husband did the destroying, remember?" the kid said, swinging the gun around.

"I did," Mason declared. "Gabe was a rapist and a criminal. His life was a complete mess, as he was regularly breaking and entering other people's homes. He came into my home to try and hurt my wife and to force me to watch," Mason shared. "What would you have done?"

"Doesn't matter. What I want is Granddad's money, and he's got a shit ton of it."

Mason snorted. "No money is left, kid. What your granddad really has is lies. Lies and the ability to con people well past all reason. The old son of a bitch is nearly broke. Yet he's got you and Steve and other guys ruining your lives, chasing money he doesn't even have."

Cristal cried out, "Listen to him. He's right. Richard never helped me with any real money all these years, and he should have. He occasionally gave me pocket money, nothing more. He should have done better than that."

Tesla nodded. "Yes, he should have. You were raising Richard's child, and Richard had the money to help back then."

"He didn't want anybody to know," she whispered. "It had to be secret, so he used to give me little bits and pieces from his petty cash. Any time the lawyers would come, he would get more spending money, and they always asked him what he was using it for. He would glare at them and tell them it was none of their damn business." She smiled at that. "But still, he was never there to help out in a way I could count on."

"He could have though," Tesla said. "He could have at any time."

"Yes, but I think he just liked playing games. He didn't want anyone to know and said it would serve them all right. He changed his will constantly, at least he talked about it all the time," she added. "I don't even know who's in it anymore. I don't know that he ever intended to give anybody his money."

"What about your son, Steve? Would Richard give him money?" Mason asked.

She winced. "I don't know what to say, but I do know right from wrong. Somewhere, somehow, that old bastard got to my Steve. He's bad, just really, really bad." She sniffled and tried to rub the tears out of her eyes. "I tried to get Richard to stay away from my grandson, after he turned my own son against me," she whispered, "but I think it was just Richard's way of punishing me for giving birth to the one son he wanted to legitimately call his own, and yet he wouldn't."

Mason stated, "Richard certainly could have. There were options. With your agreement, Richard could have added his name to the birth certificate. He even could have adopted Steve."

She stared at him with a haunted expression. "His wife didn't know."

Tesla stared at her and asked, "What about his daughters? Did they know Richard wasn't their biological father?"

"They didn't know either," Cristal confirmed, "and now

only one daughter is left, and she's dying of cancer. Richard wanted to make sure that she still had the same opinion of him after all these years, so he didn't want it to be a lie for her."

Tesla stared at her. "How will they feel when they find out about all the things that Richard's done?"

"It doesn't matter," the grandson interrupted impatiently, as he waved the gun. "Like what the hell? … I don't give a crap who and what and when or how many other people there are. As long as that will is in my name, it won't matter."

"What about your father, Steve?" Mason asked.

"My father is an ass," he snapped. "He made damn sure that I never got any support or anything I wanted in life. He was just too cocky and too mean to share."

Cristal sighed. "I'm so sorry."

"You keep saying that," he said, glaring at her, "but it doesn't matter. Don't you understand? Nothing matters, just that I get what's due to me."

"And yet I wonder if what's due to you," Mason pointed out, "is really what's due to you."

He blinked. "I don't care about your mumbo jumbo. I just need to finish the job. Granddad just needs to know, and then I get everything."

"There isn't anything to get," Cristal cried out. "That's what I keep telling you. Richard kept changing his will because it was all a game to him, but there's a reason the lawyers would only let him have so much money a month."

"Yes, because the home would take it all. If they thought he had more money, they would have charged him more," the gunman claimed, turning on her. "Can't you understand that? You just don't have a head for business at all."

He spoke to his grandmother with such a disparaging tone that Tesla snapped, "Don't you talk to your grandmother like that. She's done an awful lot to try and help you."

"Oh God," he muttered, cackling. "Another one of those goody-goody people," he said, with a sneer.

"What about your mother?" Mason asked. "How will she take this?"

"I don't give a shit how she takes it." He pointed to Tesla. "My mother's another one—although unlike this one—my mother doesn't want to bother anybody. She doesn't want any trouble and just wants to get on with her life."

"Is that so wrong?" Tesla asked.

"It sure is when I didn't get a life at all. I have every right to be what I want to be. Besides, she's got a new boyfriend, and she doesn't care."

"Did she ever have any more kids?" Tesla asked.

"No, she didn't," he said, looking at her. "Why?"

"Just wondered. And what about you? Have you got a girlfriend?" Tesla asked.

"Nope, and I won't make that same mistake," he vowed. "I will make sure that I get what I want in life first, then make sure that nobody can take it from me."

Tesla sighed, as she listened to him. "I guess all of that is really important to you, isn't it?"

"Of course it's important to me," he replied, staring at her. "Do you know what it's like to grow up without money?"

"No, I don't," she said, shaking her head. "I had a loving father and a loving brother, and now I have a loving husband," she said, looking to Mason. "But now you're the one trying to take everything away from me."

"I won't *try*. I will do it." Then he laughed. "But what you lose, I gain, so thanks." As he raised the handgun once more, his grandmother stepped in front of him.

"Nope, you'll have to kill me first."

He pointed the gun right at her chest and said, "Fine by me. You've been a pain in my ass for a very long time."

His grandmother burst into tears, wailing.

"Oh shut up!" the gunman roared. "All you ever do is bellyache." When he failed to get Cristal to shut up, he finally got frustrated enough that he put the gun against her head. "Now stop it or else."

Sobbing quietly, she managed to stop.

"Now get out of here. Just leave the room."

She stared at him.

"Yeah, leave. You don't want to know about it. You don't want to hear it, so the easiest thing for you is to just leave."

"When I leave," she whispered, "and you do this terrible deed, your life is over. It doesn't need to be over," she cried out. "It's not too late."

"Yeah, it's too late already," he argued, giving her a grim smile. "You might not have believed Granddad, but I do, and that money is mine. I need it, and I will break this cycle of poverty," he declared. "You don't want anything to do with it, and that's fine. I wasn't planning on sharing anyway." And, with that, he gave a bark of laughter, raised the handgun again, and said, "Now, make a decision."

She stared at him, then turned to look at Mason and Tesla.

He turned his gaze back to them as well, and he laughed. "Jeez, look at you guys. It's not as if you can do anything. You're just sitting here, ducks on a pond, waiting to be shot and to be put out of your misery," he muttered. "It's almost too easy."

As he turned the gun to Mason, Markus launched from the floor and tightened his arm around the gunman's neck, threw him off balance, and grabbed his gun arm, pulling the gun free at the same time. As he flipped him onto his stomach, he came down on his back, a knee digging hard into the boy's spine.

Cristal burst into tears, sobbing and wailing at the sudden turn of events. Tesla got up, waddled over to her, and she wrapped her arms around her and whispered, "It's okay. It's okay now."

Cristal shook her head. "It's never okay," she whispered. "These men, they just …" And then she couldn't continue and just burst into tears all over again, but Tesla understood.

She looked over at Mason, and he nodded. She just held Cristal, then asked her, "What about his mother?"

She looked over at him and whispered, "His mother doesn't have anything to do with this. She's a good person. It took a lot for her to recover, but now she's put herself through school, and she's done well. She has a new relationship, and I wondered if maybe that would be better for her son, but instead he blames her still."

"It's easier to blame people," Tesla explained, "than it is to deal with your own problems. But good for her for managing to move on, after Steve abandoned her and their child." Tesla looked over at Markus and smiled. "You must have one hell of a headache."

He groaned. "It stunned me for a moment, though it pisses me off that this dumb kid got by me. I will blame it all on your damn food."

She laughed. "I watched you playing possum, waiting for

an opportunity," she noted, "so you are as strategic as ever."

"As if I would let this snot-nosed kid shoot you," Markus muttered, with an eye roll. "As you well know, I can move like a cat when I need to. You guys had him talking, so it was better to get as much information as we could because he sure won't talk now."

His grandmother still sobbed, but then she stopped and looked around wildly. "He might not talk, but I will. This has to stop," she cried out. "My grandson's just poison, like Steve and like Richard."

"The old man has already been picked up and is sitting in jail," Mason shared. "So now it's over."

Cristal stared at him in hope. "You promise? So many people have died or have had their lives ruined because of him."

"It's over," Mason repeated. "I promise."

And, with that, Cristal sagged into a heap on the floor, rolled her head onto her knees, and just sobbed some more.

Markus looked at Mason, then Tesla, and added, "I think you may be right. This thing is finally over."

CHAPTER 7

TESLA WALKED INTO her house, just as Markus pulled up behind them and unloaded the groceries and a few other things they might need. Jasper had Mason in another vehicle, and they slowly pulled in behind, bringing Mason home for the very first time in many weeks. Sebastian and her father would arrive in an hour or so. She couldn't wait. She'd finally have her family back together and all home. Tesla smiled with joy, as everybody pitched in to help settle them back into their house again. As she stood here, staring at her husband slowly walking into the room, Jasper came up beside her.

"Are you okay?" he asked.

She smiled, hugged him, and whispered, "I'm doing just fine now."

"And the baby?"

"And baby's fine too. I wondered a couple times if I would go into early labor," she admitted, with a shake of her head, "but I'm very grateful that he is holding off."

"He?" Jasper asked in a teasing voice. "I thought it was a girl this time?"

"We don't know for sure, but that's what I'm saying now," she shared, with a chuckle. "Regardless, I just want a healthy baby. We will love this child whether it's a boy or a girl. Now that I have Mason home, that's what counts. That's what is important."

Jasper nodded. "It's been a pretty rough go."

"It has been," she stated, "but it's okay now." He raised his eyebrows, but she nodded. "It really is okay. I know that we've had a lot of craziness, but sometimes that craziness needs to happen for everybody to calm down and to get to the bottom of it."

"What we had was just poisonous men, carrying on their tirade of fear and torment until they were seriously done. The latest news is, Richard had a heart attack. I don't know if he's *done*, really done for, but he won't be causing any trouble."

"I'm hoping we can get the last little bits of information from him before he goes," she replied, "if only for cleaning up the case on record. I know that's what everybody's hoping for. In the meantime, there's an awful lot of paperwork to catch up on."

Jasper grinned and nodded. "At least I have a team now that I can trust beyond all doubt, and I can assign them to take care of things discreetly."

She rolled her eyes at that. "Don't tell me that you will try and get out of doing paperwork."

"Of course I will," he admitted, with a big grin. "We all deserve some time off after this one."

"And you will get some of that time off yourself, right?" she asked pointedly.

"Yes, we will all get it," he confirmed. "Not to worry."

"Good. I don't want anything to happen to you either."

"Nothing will happen to me," Jasper noted. "Besides, there might be a wedding coming up—after you have the baby, of course."

"What?" She stared at him. "Really? You're getting married?"

"Yep."

"Oh, Jasper, that's wonderful."

"The way I hear it, there may be a few other weddings coming up too."

She smiled. "I sure hope that Guilliam and Janelle are on that list."

"I expect so," Jasper replied. "I would give them all a week or two of rest and recuperation, but I won't be surprised if the wedding announcements start rolling in pretty quickly. Nothing like nearly losing someone special to all of us to remind people to make the best of each moment they have," Jasper shared.

She nodded. "I would definitely agree with that. Look at the two of us." With a smile, she looked back at Mason, sitting in his favorite living room chair.

"He will be okay now, right?" Jasper asked in concern.

"He will be better than okay," she declared, with a smile, "and thank you for bringing this to an end."

"You're welcome, and thank you for bringing me back here."

"I'm so glad you came," she whispered, as she hugged him. "Family is everything."

When the other guys left, she walked over to Mason and suggested, "I think you need to get some rest." When he waggled his eyebrows, she chuckled. "Oh no, none of that."

"Oh, I don't know about that," he argued, with a flirty smile.

"Between the two of us, I'm not sure either of us is ready," she noted.

His smile fell away, and he released a big sigh. "I was so worried about you."

"Oh, I'm fine," she said, chuckling, as she rubbed her baby belly, "but I won't be upset when this stage is over either."

"Of course not," he agreed, as he gently stroked her belly, feeling the baby moving.

"Have you thought about what you will do now to keep you busy and in line with following doctor's orders?" she asked.

"Nope. I'll just wait and see what happens."

"Are you sure about that?"

"Yeah, I'm sure," he declared, with a careless wave.

She reminded him of that when they made their way slowly to bed that night.

When he stretched out for the first time in his own bed, he groaned. "Dear God, this feels amazing."

"I know," she murmured, as she crawled in behind him. "Nothing quite like home, is there?"

"No, there isn't," he agreed, as he tucked her up close. "Or this." He just held her close and muttered, "Now for some sleep."

EPILOGUE

MASON DID GET several hours in, but somewhere in the early morning he got a phone call. He woke up, saw the number on the phone, and frowned. Slipping out of bed, he walked to the window and answered it. "Sir?"

"How are you?" retired Navy Commander Doran Magellan asked formally.

"I just made it home from the hospital, so I would say I'm somewhat okay," Mason replied in a dry tone.

"Right, I guess I should have waited a little longer, *huh*?"

"Knowing you, sir, I suspect that, for you, this *is* waiting a little longer."

Doran boomed with laughter, and he replied, "Yeah, you got that right. Anyway I'll let you get back to your wife."

"Maybe you should explain why you called in the first place."

"I just wanted to know if you were up for a special job."

His eyebrows shot up. "Do I get a chance to recuperate?"

"*Ha*, I figured you'd recuperated enough already."

"Per the doc, I have another couple weeks," he noted carefully, masking his tone, "but, once I'm cleared for work, I'm definitely interested."

"How about you come see me in two weeks?"

Mason groaned. "What if I need more than two weeks?"

"Okay, that's pushing it, but, if you say so, I'll wait," Doran noted drily, "but I can't wait too long."

"So, what's the job?"

"I don't want to give you too many details in case you're not up for it."

"Now you're just being an ass, sir, and teasing me."

"Yeah," Doran agreed, with a chuckle. "I want you to say yes, but I need to know that you're capable of handling the job."

"I wouldn't say yes if I wasn't capable," Mason said in exasperation, "and it's not as if I need anything more than some time to heal physically."

"Are you sure?"

"I'm sure," Mason stated forcefully.

"Good. You're hired."

"Doesn't mean I want the job. I don't even know what it is, remember?"

"You want the job."

"Now why is that?"

"Because I want you to head up a special division."

"I'm not sure that I'm up for doing too many missions, too far away, especially considering we have a baby due soon."

"Right, I forgot about that. How's Tesla doing?"

"She's doing great." Mason chuckled. "What's that got to do with anything?"

"Maybe nothing," Doran conceded, "but you can probably do all the management from town."

"In that case, I'm interested, but you still haven't told me anything about it."

"Nope, I haven't, but you've already said yes, so that's

good enough for me. I'll touch base in a while." And, with that, he terminated the call.

Staring down at his phone, Mason groaned and made his way back to the bed.

Tesla murmured, "What did he want?"

"He wants me to head up a special division," he shared, with a note of laughter, since she'd clearly figured out the identity of the caller.

Her eyes flew open. "You're not healthy enough for that yet."

"Yeah, but he's giving me a couple weeks to get *healthy enough*," he added, still chuckling.

"What kind of special division?"

"That's the problem. He didn't say."

"Oh, hell no," she stated, sitting up now. "That could have you in all kinds of trouble."

"It could," he agreed, "but it does keep life interesting. Besides, … how bad could it be?"

"With him? It could be bad," she muttered. "*Special division* sounds like black ops to me."

"Sure, and you know that the Mavericks are shut down."

"I heard that," she muttered. "I think Doran mentioned it somewhere along the line. So, maybe it's something like that?"

"I don't know, but I've got to tell you, sweetie, I am interested."

She groaned. "Of course you are. If it keeps you home and if it keeps you out of trouble, I'm all for it. However, if it means you will bum around the world, getting into shit constantly, I can't say I'm a big fan."

He pulled her closer into his arms. "He said I could stay close."

She shifted up on one elbow and frowned.

Mason nodded. "His words."

"*Hmm*," she muttered. "Doran does know that he will have to talk to me about it before you say okay, right?"

He burst out laughing. "I think he is fully aware that whatever I decide will be a joint decision on our part."

"Except you already said yes."

"He didn't tell me the details, so it's not as if he will hold me to it, especially if it's not something I want to do."

She laughed. "Look at you. You're already beaming. It's clearly something you want to do, but maybe you should find out a little more before you fully commit."

"Oh, I'll find out when he's ready to tell me," Mason noted, with a chuckle, as he wrapped his arms around her again. "How about you go back to sleep? You sound like you could use a little more rest."

"Ha," she replied, "you're just changing the topic."

"I am," he admitted. "Is it working?"

"No," she declared, as she hugged him closer and whispered, "But you can keep trying."

He lowered his head and kissed her, then murmured, "I thought this wasn't allowed."

"It's probably not," she noted, "but maybe we can get creative."

He groaned softly and whispered, "Oh, I promise that I can get very creative."

"And gentle too."

"Absolutely," he whispered, as he slowly stroked her body, murmuring over the changes since he'd been gone.

"It was bad enough that you went up north, leaving me alone for months, but then to get shot coming off the plane? Who does that for a homecoming?" she asked.

"I know. I'm so sorry about that."

"Of course you're sorry, but it's not your fault."

"No, apparently it was the fault of an awful lot of people though," he noted, "and that's okay because it's over." When he finally slid into her from behind, then held her close, she shuddered in his arms. All too soon he shuddered through his release too. After his breathing returned to normal, he whispered, "Just this, just holding you like this, … it's everything."

"I know," she whispered. "I'm so damn glad to have you back, but I still want to know more before you commit to this special assignment."

He smiled as he held her close. He'd already committed, and she would be all on board when she knew. Yet she was right. It was time to commit to spending more time with family and to keeping safe everything he held dear, but that didn't mean he couldn't be out there, doing a whole lot more to keep the rest of the world safe too.

Still entwined, Mason and Tesla both fell back asleep, enjoying what would now be the rest of their lives, in peace and hopefully in harmony forever.

This concludes Book 6 of Man Down: Mason's Mark.
Read about Rubin: Mason's Aces, Book 1

Sneak Peek for Rubin
Mason's Aces
Book 1

COMMANDER MASON CALLISTER stared out the window, his hands crossed behind his back. On this first day in his brand-new office, the room felt empty and hollow. It wasn't his yet; he didn't fit the space, and neither did the space fit him. Mason heard a noise behind him, several other noises going on around him, inside and outside. It would take a bit to get used to the new location, to the larger office, and to the huge desk—as if the size were in direct proportion to the power he now wielded. And then there was the title, … plus the responsibility that went with it. But, to Mason, it was more about the priceless intangibles that this office represented. He stared down at his hands, wondering whether he was good enough for this.

It was a new stage—a new beginning. It had been months since he'd been released from the hospital, a time in which Tesla had given birth to their second child, an absolutely gorgeous daughter, and he couldn't have been happier. During those months, he had managed several times to push back retired Navy Commander Doran Magellan until Doran had finally said, "No more waiting."

So here Mason was, facing another turning point in his

career. Sure, Doran had said that Mason could go out on missions anytime he wanted, but he also knew that things were changing. *He* was changing. In truth, it was time for a change. Black Ops but not. Special Division but not. He was curious to see how this new beginning would turn out. Doran would say it was no different than all the work Mason had been doing for decades. So the same but different.

Doran was Mason's sole boss, but no one could know. Doran was the only one with full knowledge of what Mason was doing—the why, the where, the who. He glanced down at his watch. In fifteen minutes, his handpicked team would arrive, men who he had worked with, men who he trusted.

The trouble was, he still didn't necessarily understand what *this* was. Doran had left this team's overall mission guidelines very open, just saying it was Special Ops, and he needed Mason to head it. But then this morning, Doran sent a message that he needed Mason *now*, today, to pick a team, to be ready to go immediately, and to expect that to be the norm from now on.

Mason shook his head, wondering how he could go from the peace and quiet, the joy and solitude at his wife's side, adoring their newest addition to their family, and then jump right into this organized chaos. Yet he also knew that he wouldn't have been called if there hadn't been a need. And, whenever there was a need, he would always step up.

He did this work not just for his wife and for his children but for every other American as well. It was for a better future. It was for the highest good of the country. His commitment was there, front and center, always.

He gave a heavy sigh, as he turned to face the desk. His assistant would be in soon, also somebody Mason had worked with previously. And that was part of his conditional acceptance, that Mason's men came first and foremost, that he had a team he could trust, that his people had his back as he navigated this new world. He'd made that abundantly clear. Doran had no qualms about giving Mason a free hand on that aspect either. Doran had agreed immediately, telling Mason to pick whomever he wanted. And that was a good thing. Mason had already picked the team for this first assignment.

He didn't even know what this initial op was. Yet now he would be in that need-to-know loop. Details were on their way to him right now. Such a strange place to be, but one that he, in a way, was more comfortable with. The transparency of need-to-know also meant that Mason would deal with any related problems. That was a change. That would be, in some ways, challenging. Yet his actions would be double-checked by him and by him only, to confirm that he had the power to do what needed to be done.

No more red tape, no more battles for funds, for agreements, for signatures, all designed to put a monkey wrench in real-life problem-solving. Doran had assured Mason that his division would walk in the shadows, answering to no one but Doran, the man himself being the master of living in the dark. Maybe Mason should be worried about that.

And then again maybe not. Maybe it was for the best if none of them knew how this worked on Doran's end. Because, dear God, when too many hands were in the pot, nothing ever got done. And Mason was a doer in this world, one, when assigned a task, who had it done on time, if not three hours early. And this would be no different. Mason looked forward to no more fights for equipment, for training, for all the things needed to make an optimum team more successful.

Just then came a knock on the door. He turned and called out, "Come in."

His assistant poked his head inside, smiled, and came in with a thick file and six stapled copies, which he placed on the desk.

Mason nodded at his old friend Jeremy, somebody who had walked away from the field quite a few years ago after a couple major close calls came with injuries that kept him at a desk. This new position would still keep him doing what he loved the most, which was helping this country.

"Six, right?" he asked Mason.

"Yes, six for now, but I expect to have a total team of twelve, at least to start."

"Good enough. If you want to give me the additional names, we can brief them now too."

"Not yet," Mason murmured. "Not until I see just what the scope of this one will be."

Jeremy sighed. "It'll be bad."

"Hell, they're all bad." If they weren't, no need to bring in Mason and his team.

"It's always that way, and it always will be that way," Jeremy agreed. "That's one of the reasons we do what we do because nobody else can do this. It takes people like us. And that's why I'm happy to be here serving with you, sir." With a smile and a nod, Jeremy turned, opened the door, and let in the handpicked team.

Mason smiled as he studied the men as they entered. Mason had worked with these men in some of the most appalling conditions, where each one had steadfastly shown who they were, even in the worst of times.

"Take a seat, gentlemen. We don't have much time. Review the briefs Jeremy is handing out. And let's get started."

Find Book 1 here!

To find out more visit Dale Mayer's website.

https://geni.us/DMSMARubin

Rubin: Mason's Aces (Book #1)

Welcome to a captivating new series by USA Today bestselling author Dale Mayer. Reconnect with old friends and meet new ones as Mason sets off on another exhilarating journey. With a fresh department, a dynamic team, and countless thrilling adventures, immerse yourself in the action, as Mason and his Aces work to save the world …

When Mason put out the call to assemble a covert black ops team, Rubin hesitated. But his friend Trent insisted, promising a break from the monotony of red tape and brass BS. With a leap of faith, Rubin entrusted his fate to Mason, unaware of the chaos that awaited …

Tricia was on the cusp of completing her master's degree, her future bright, when a night out turned into a nightmare. As she returned to her dorm, shadows closed in, and she was thrust into a van with two other captives. Her world spiraled into chaos, leaving her questioning if she was a target or simply a victim of cruel chance.

Then Rubin appeared. Seizing the moment, Tricia escaped her captors, but the path to safety was fraught with peril and unexpected twists. As danger loomed, an undeniable connection sparked between Tricia and Rubin, turning their escape into a journey of suspense and burgeoning romance …

Find Book 1 here!
To find out more visit Dale Mayer's website.
https://geni.us/DMSMARubin

Author's Note

Thank you for reading Mason's Mark: Man Down, Book 6! If you enjoyed the book, please take a moment and leave a short review.

Dear reader,

I love to hear from readers, and you can contact me at my website: www.dalemayer.com or at my Facebook author page. To be informed of new releases and special offers, sign up for my newsletter or follow me on BookBub. And if you are interested in joining Dale Mayer's Reader Group, here is the Facebook sign up page.
http://geni.us/DaleMayerFBGroup

Cheers,
Dale Mayer

About the Author

Dale Mayer is a *USA Today* best-selling author, best known for her SEALs military romances, her Psychic Visions series, and her Lovely Lethal Garden cozy series. Her contemporary romances are raw and full of passion and emotion (Broken But … Mending, Hathaway House series). Her thrillers will keep you guessing (Kate Morgan, By Death series), and her romantic comedies will keep you giggling (*It's a Dog's Life*, a stand-alone novella; and the Broken Protocols series, starring Charming Marvin, the cat).

Dale honors the stories that come to her—and some of them are crazy, break all the rules and cross multiple genres!

To go with her fiction, she also writes nonfiction in many different fields, with books available on résumé writing, companion gardening, and the US mortgage system. All her books are available in print and ebook format.

Connect with Dale Mayer Online

Dale's Website – www.dalemayer.com
Twitter – @DaleMayer
Facebook Page – geni.us/DaleMayerFBFanPage
Facebook Group – geni.us/DaleMayerFBGroup
BookBub – geni.us/DaleMayerBookbub
Instagram – geni.us/DaleMayerInstagram
Goodreads – geni.us/DaleMayerGoodreads
Newsletter – geni.us/DaleNews